THE HOUND OF TRURAN

When Beth, a nurse in Singapore, is tragically orphaned, she feels she needs to get away. She takes a job in a large country house in Cornwall, but things don't go smoothly; a mad woman in the house tries to get rid of her, a ghost dog keeps appearing, and a wayward sister runs off with the man Beth was hoping to marry. However, the young nurse finally discovers love where she least expects it.

BARBARA BEST

◆

THE HOUND OF TRURAN

Complete and Unabridged

LINFORD
Leicester

First Linford Edition
published September 1994

British Library CIP Data

Best, Barbara
The hound of Truran.—Large print ed.—
Linford romance library
I. Title II. Series
823 [F]

ISBN 0–7089–7601–8

Published by
F. A. Thorpe (Publishing) Ltd.
Anstey, Leicestershire

Set by Words & Graphics Ltd.
Anstey, Leicestershire
Printed and bound in Great Britain by
T. J. Press (Padstow) Ltd., Padstow, Cornwall

This book is printed on acid-free paper

1

THE tattered fronds of the palm trees whispered together in the early evening breeze and the cicadas shrieked their nocturnal chorus, but the girl, seated in the small study, was quite unaware of the gathering dusk or its mystery, her pencil poised over an untidy sheaf of papers, a frown puckering her forehead. An open letter lay to her right.

What should she do, thought Beth distractedly, leaning her head on her hand, her fingers ruffling through the dark hair that held more than a hint of copper in its silky depths, a sure sign of her inner perturbation. The letter, from her godmother almost demanded that she spend a holiday with her in Cornwall. Beth fingered her pencil restlessly. She would like to visit Mrs. Trevelgen, but should she pull up all her roots here? She had made many friends and was now a respected sister at the big hospital on the hill.

However, there was Fenella, her eighteen year old sister. In fact, Beth felt it her duty, now that their parents were dead, to provide a home for Fenella, but how could she leave Singapore and Kim?

Trapped by her uncertainty and warring loyalties, Beth felt the burden of responsibility heavy on her young shoulders. If only she knew what Kim was going to do, but he, himself, was unsettled and had said, on more than one occasion, when she had tried to pin him down to something concrete, that as soon as he had passed through medical school, he would seek pastures new, but where?

Ah Wing, the old Malay woman, who had been with the Dexter family for twenty-three years, came into the room. She was small, with nut brown skin and grey flecked black hair, drawn back primly from a wrinkled face.

"Tuan Crudden on the phone," disapproval in every line of that shrivelled body.

"Oh good!" said Beth, springing up from her chair. It would be a relief to be able to shelve her problems for even a few minutes. "*Amah!*" she called as she replaced the receiver on its cradle, "Tuan Kim will be here for supper."

Ah Wing followed Beth to the bedroom, a frown adding to the deep furrows on her brow.

"I don't like it, Missie," she said in her forthright way, picking up the dress Beth had carelessly thrown across the cane chair and putting it neatly on a hanger. "This young man — why can't there be an announcement?"

Beth laughed happily as she slipped a fresh frock over her head, pulling it down over her slim hips.

"But *amah*, you'll be here. Everything will be all right."

"But the announcement?" persisted Ah Wing stubbornly. "Why isn't there an announcement?"

3

"I've told you before," Beth said patiently. "Tuan Kim wants to pass his exams before we announce our engagement. Why doesn't that satisfy you?"

"You should have been engaged long ago, Missie Beth, and the wedding could have come when the *tuan* has become a doctor. I'm worrying about you now that the *tuan* and the *mem* are dead. Who is there to look after you but Ah Wing?"

"Please go and get the supper," she said gently, "and don't worry about me. By the way," her young voice called out. "I've had a letter from Mem Trevelgen — you remember her? She came and stayed here? Now she wants me to go to England and visit her."

Ah Wing poked her withered body around the door again, small brown eyes bright, her smile revealing betel stained teeth.

"Missie Beth will go?" she asked eagerly.

"I don't know, *amah*. I just don't

4

know what to do."

"It's the *tuan*, isn't it?" said Ah Wing shrewdly. "What kind of a lover is he? You should be as glowing and happy as the honey bird in the garden, but all the *tuan* does, is make you worried. It's not good. He's not the man for you, Missie."

Beth swung round, hair brush suspended half way up to her head.

"Ah Wing! How can you say such a thing!"

The old Malay's eyes were tender as they rested on the indignant face in front of her. "It's the truth I say. You know as well as I do, Missie Beth, that Tuan Kim is one who flits from flower to flower, sipping, but never drawing deep. You must go to your godmother, the Mem Trevelgen. She will look after you well."

Half an hour later, Beth opened the door to a well-knit, athletic figure, who immediately took her in his arms and held her close.

"You always look so sweet and

5

fresh," he muttered into her silky hair. "I feel I can be at rest when I'm with you and heaven alone knows, I need it."

Beth led the way into the lounge, her hand curled in his, her head turned towards him as she laughingly said:

"Someone been difficult this afternoon?"

Kim went across to the cabinet and poured out two drinks.

"We won't talk shop," he said firmly.

Beth watched the bent head, a catch in her throat and her heart in her eyes. How very dear he was. All her fears and uncertainties took wing when she was with him. Fair hair, a handful falling untidily across a high forehead, had been bleached almost white from the Singapore sun and sea. His medium height and hazel eyes made up the picture of this energetic young medical student who, Beth's friends insisted, she had only fallen in love with because he was so absolutely opposite to her own darker colouring.

She had laughingly agreed for it

had been that fair head that had first attracted her attention her heart turning over painfully at the sight of him. A Saxon god, she had likened him to, standing out in a room of dark haired, dark skinned people.

Her best friend had opened her brown eyes wide when Kim had first asked Beth to go out with him. Disbelief had mingled with acute astonishment.

"Darling, congrats! Everyone of us will be green with envy!" She had gone on to enumerate Kim's good points. "Handsome, has his own yacht, swims like a porpoise and as for his dancing — ." She had left the sentence unfinished to roll mischievous eyes ceilingward.

Beth had smiled.

"The shock has been almost as great for me, Meg."

"Oh, I don't know," Meg answered with a considering look. "You're such a nice person, Beth. I'm surprised Kim Crudden noticed, that's all. He usually likes his packages exotically wrapped

7

and doesn't delve into what isn't the obvious."

How had it happened? That was the question Beth was to ask herself many times as Kim continued to date her.

Meg's honest brown eyes, watching Beth's happy face, grew more and more troubled as the days grew into months, for Kim was notorious for the number of girls he had taken out.

Beth had smilingly gone her own way, burying her own doubts and fears deep in her heart; the terrible uncertainty that one day the phone would ring and the excuses begin. That was four months ago.

Kim was now handing her a glass of fresh orange juice which he knew Beth liked at this hour of the day.

"You don't know how pleased I was when you phoned," she said lightly.

"Love me still?" his eyes on the sweep of her throat.

Beth nodded.

"Haven't I always, since that very first glimpse of you at that hospital dance?" She sighed, but quickly caught it back, sipping her drink. Kim wanted a gay companion, not one that kept looking over her shoulder.

"Supper," announced Ah Wing briefly from the open doorway, her dark eyes hooded.

"I don't think *amah* likes me," said Kim, pulling out a chair for Beth.

"She just thinks it is not quite the thing for you to be calling on me now that — " swallowing quickly "since Mum and Dad — " Beth could not go on, keeping her eyes lowered as Ah Wing served them.

"If only there was some definite news," Beth said tightly. "They could have been driven into one of a hundred small inlets, the yacht crippled — not able to get back home."

"Yes," he conceded gently, "but Beth, it is over two months ago and an extensive search has been made."

Beth pushed her plate away. Her appetite had completely deserted her, grey eyes darkening as she recalled again that dreadful day when her parents had been caught in a sudden gale while out yachting. She had come home for her off duty, the storm breaking an hour later with a ferocity quite common to this part of the world and had sat in the lounge, the shutters battened down against the onslaught, wondering anxiously if her parents had found safe harbourage before the gale had struck.

Near midnight, Beth had gone back to the hospital only a few minutes walk away.

Matron had been most kind and had rung up the authorities, notifying them of Mr. and Mrs. Dexter's plight. That, as Kim had just said, was over two months ago.

Beth was recalled to the present by Kim saying gently: "Come back, sweetie."

She laughed a little tremulously and when they were once more seated comfortably in the lounge told him about the letter she had received from her godmother.

"She wants me to go to Cornwall for a while and there is Fen to consider."

Kim turned to her quickly, the tawny-green eyes eager under their sandy overlay.

"Darling, I hope you accepted by return post. This is just what you need — a complete break from all this."

Had he been too eager, wondered Beth, and tried to dismiss the unworthy thought. "I'll have to leave this house soon, anyway. The company has been very good in allowing me to stay on so long and Fen seems to think she would like to settle in England, so perhaps it would be a good idea if I did go over there as well," looking at him warily, her eyes anxious. "Kim, what are your plans?"

He got up restlessly, hands deep in his pockets.

"Well, as you know, I don't want to stay on here, when I have passed my finals."

It was typical of the man, thought Beth, that he had no fears of not making the grade. Some people called him cocky and would have liked to have seen him take a tumble. That was the price of popularity, but Beth knew he also possessed a deep, burning obsession to heal, she also knew, to her cost, that even when Kim got his degree, he would certainly not settle down in any one place.

Beth pushed the thought aside. What if Kim hadn't all the more solid virtues? She loved him, she told herself firmly, but he surprised her when he said gaily.

"London is as good a place as any in which to make a start, I guess. If I don't like it, we can always try somewhere else. Once I'm qualified the world will be our oyster, darling," coming back to sit beside her.

"Oh Kim!" breathed Beth, laying her head against him, a wide happy smile lighting her face, all the tension gone. "When did you make up your mind — to try for a job in London, I mean?"

"Now, this very minute," his glance arrogant.

Beth had to laugh. All her problems had miraculously ironed themselves out. She would write to her godmother, tonight and accept her invitation, stay in Cornwall for a few days then find herself a job in London and a flat where she would be able to welcome Fenella and find out just what her sister wanted to do in the way of a career. Her letters of late had jumped from one fancied occupation to another like a puppet on a string.

A week later Kim drove Beth to the airport. She paused before stepping into the car, taking a silent farewell of the house and garden she had known all her life. It had been a sad parting with Ah Wing earlier that day, knowing that she would never again see the old *amah*, as she would no more be made aware of the heady perfume of frangipani and chempaka flowers, or the fragrance of sandalwood, spices and dried fish, that was so much a part of Singapore.

"Come along, Beth," urged Kim impatiently. "Can't have you miss that plane," rattling the handle of the door he was holding open for her.

Beth slid into the seat, staring out of the window through a mist of tears, at the familiar and well-loved streets, as they drove down town; the shops with their Chinese characters, the conglomeration of different races, picking out an old woman here, in black trousers, blue jacket and wide brimmed straw hat, a young woman there in a figure-hugging *cheongsum*, in beautifully embroidered cream satin, a red flower in her dark hair, holding them all in her memory, storing them away carefully.

At the airport, after all the usual formalities, she stood waiting for her flight to be called, her hand held tightly in Kim's.

"You'll write?" she said through stiff

lips, her eyes suddenly blurring again.

"Of course I will, darling," he promised. "The weeks will just slip by you'll see. There, your flight has been called." He pulled her into his arms, kissing her long and deeply.

The 'plane rose steeply into the night sky, the airport buildings rushing by and there below them lay Singapore, a lovely sight, the street lights rows of glittering necklaces of precious gems, the sea a black, mysterious shadow.

Beth was not a good traveller and the hours dragged by in a kind of haze. If only she could sleep, but this was denied her. Her thoughts circled around Kim, Ah Wing, her godmother, that kindly person who had made the long trip to Singapore to see them.

It had been a happy visit, Beth remembered and now she would be seeing her godmother again. What was her family like?

Suspended in that half way state between reality and dreams, Beth suddenly found herself on a platform of a railway station, running after a man, her high heels making it impossible to close the gap between them. She had to warn him about something and sobbed with frustration as she tried frantically to will her legs to carry her, as that dark head moved through the dense crowd and then, with a whimper of horror, saw him board the train. Fighting her way through the crowd, fear rasping in her throat, threatening to choke her, Beth found she had not moved an inch; tried to scream, but only a whisper came from her dry lips. It was too late. The train was already drawing out of the station.

Beth had not glimpsed the face of the man, but he was someone she loved with all her heart and being. He was part of her and in some dreadful danger; knew if she lost him, it would be the end of the world for her.

A deep sense of loss spilled through her as the last carriage disappeared down the line and did not find it at all strange, that it was not Kim's fair head that had just eluded her.

The platform faded and Beth saw the accident. A higgledy-piggledy trail of crumpled coaches lay scattered alongside the railway line. The Station clock read *30th June*.

Beth awoke, shivering violently, to find the hostess bending over her, a gentle hand shaking her shoulder.

"Are you all right, Madam?" she was asking anxiously.

Beth sat up, her hand trembling over her wet forehead, her words coming out jerkily.

"Yes, it — it was just a bad dream."

"I'll bring you a cup of tea." The hostess spoke soothingly.

The hot tea refreshed Beth and good sense told her that her haggard reflection in the small mirror in the toilet would disappear after a real night's rest, but it did nothing to cheer her up and she longed for this trip to end.

London airport at last and Beth thankfully walked away from the aircraft with a firm conviction that flying, as far as she was concerned, was not for the likes of her. The bus took her into the city where she booked in at an hotel and after a meal and a hot bath, was soon asleep.

The following morning Beth was her old self again and was able to enjoy the many sights London had to offer, but shivered miserably in the cutting March wind that howled and danced like some dervish amongst the mixture of old and new buildings and decided that a much thicker coat was an absolute necessity. The heat of Singapore must have made her blood thinner than she realized.

Beth chose a coat of russet in a knobbly weave and huddled gratefully into its warmth. She also bought two warm dresses, one in spring green, the other in beige, both colours warming to the copper tints of her hair.

Later Beth slipped into a Post Office and sent cables to Kim, Ah Wing and Fenella and a telegram to her godmother, telling them of her safe arrival.

"St. Geraint! St. Geraint!" droned a porter the following morning.

Beth had slept soundly all night, but for the past hour had eagerly watched the countryside flash by.

The train with a clank and a hiss, drew to a halt. Beth quickly pulled out her suitcase from under the bunk and stepped on to the platform, looking around her expectantly, but nobody came to claim her.

She stood shivering, clutching her coat more closely around her slim body, watching the train sweep the bend like some giant millipede. Perhaps her telegram hadn't arrived.

The station clock jerked the minutes away and then, picking up her suitcase, Beth asked the porter how far it was to Truran. It was obvious that no one was going to meet her.

"Truran now? A couple of miles, maybe," the man said vaguely, scratching a stubbly chin with a none too clean finger. "You wanting a taxi, Miss?"

"Yes, please," Beth said with sudden decision.

In a matter of minutes, she was warmly ensconced in the front seat of a small car, the heater working wonders on her cold toes. Beth leaned forward eagerly, trying to peer through the shrouds of thin mist. Farm land had opened up, the houses, those that she could see, all made from the same local grey stone, and even the roofs were grey. A sudden hunger for colourful Singapore came over her, but she stifled the ache that home had conjured up as the driver said curiously, his small, dark eyes, under the greasy cap, coming around to rest on her for a moment.

"Going to Truran for a holiday, are you, Miss? Bit early aren't you?"

Beth smiled, liking the strong Cornish accent.

"I'm going to stay at Truran House. Do you know the Trevelgen family?" The porter's 'a couple of miles' had already turned into ten.

"Oh ay! I know Ruan and Gawen well." His wrinkled, weather-beaten face puckered with gloomy relish. "I've known them from the times they were young 'uns. Now there was a pair! Ruan, especially."

He changed into low gear for they were nosing down a winding, very steep and narrow road and then suddenly, around a sharp bend, Beth saw the village of Truran, built snugly into the bowl of the bay, the houses, once again, grey-slated, but the cobwalls were the colour of rich clotted cream.

She gazed down in delight at the completely unspoiled, picturesque little village, the fishing boats laying well up on the sugar brown beach.

The driver stopped and pointed up at the house, half veiled in a robe of mist, rising from the promontory jutting out on the far side of the cove.

"I'm afraid I'll have to drop you here, lady. This car of mine will never make that steep incline." He patted the steering wheel undismayed at the vehicle's foibles. "You could 'phone the House and ask someone to come and fetch you." His eyes again slewed around to meet hers and Beth saw he had stopped, conveniently, just outside the Post Office.

The mist had lifted a little, intermittent streaks of sunshine filtering through, picking out the bronze and green lichen on the cliffs.

"I think I'll walk, thank you," laying her fare into the calloused brown hand.

"It's further than you think, Miss," he warned as he opened the door for her and deposited her luggage on the narrow sidewalk. "It's a tidy step up there."

Beth picked up her case. It would do her good, she decided, to stretch her legs, but the old taxi driver had been quite right. The incline was steeper than she had bargained for.

Half way up, Beth was thankful to sit down on a large boulder, her gaze drawn again to the rugged outline of the coast and then on up to rest finally on the house itself, still a long way off. It looked as if it had been carved from the rock on which it stood, so deeply embedded did it appear to be.

Beth wondered again about the family with whom she would be staying. She knew there were two sons, twins, Ruan and Gawen. Gawen was married and from what she could remember, had one small son.

A fresh cloud had come off the sea and with it a fine drizzle and Beth turned with relief to watch a car coming up the steep road. It came to a halt opposite her and a surprised face popped itself out from a hastily turned down window.

"Like a lift?" and when she nodded, the man opened the far door, then sprang out to seize her case and deposit it deftly on the back seat.

"I'm just going to Truran House. I believe that's it up there," she said at his look of enquiry when he was once more behind the wheel.

"Don't tell me you're our Beth. We've been wondering when you would be arriving."

Beth turned to him quickly.

"I did send a telegram."

"I've just been down for the post. That's it in the cubby-hole, if I'm not mistaken," pointing to an orange envelope peeping out from under an assortment of letters and bills.

"But I sent it off yesterday morning," she said with dismay.

"Things are slow down here. By the way, how come I found you walking?"

"The taxi couldn't make this hill."

The man snorted.

"That's old Craddock, I bet. A proper rogue if there ever was one! He looks after that car of his as he would a baby. Not get up this hill!"

Beth's smile was mischievous.

"Yes, he said he knew Ruan and Gawen," and saw an answering grin.

"He knows us all right, and I'll have something to say when next I see him. Might as well introduce myself. I'm

24

Gawen Trevelgen." His whole manner radiated geniality.

He was a thickset man with one of those blue chins that always appear to be in need of a shave and surprisingly sensitive hands for one of his build. Thick hair, as black as an apple pip, grew back from a broad forehead and his eyes were a bright inquisitive blue.

They turned into a walled estate, through wrought iron gates, up another sharp, steep bend and stopped on a terrace. Beth looked around her with interest. The thick, grey stone walls of the house and its surrounds were bleak in the extreme, the swirling scarves of mist doing nothing to dispel this illusion. There were no shrubs or even flowers to lighten the effect, only a few trees standing crookedly, as if the wind had been too much for them.

"No money for a gardener, I'm afraid," said Gawen, who had caught her look of surprise. "We're only now recovering from enormous death duties."

Beth climbed out of the car in a kind of daze. How anyone could live without some colour around them was past her comprehension.

"Go inside," said Gawen, bending over the front seat to retrieve Beth's case, but she paused a moment to look up at the coat of arms emblazoned on the stone work above the door frame. *Take and hold, 1795* it read.

Gawen had come up behind her and opened the massive oak door with its huge brass knocker and ornate hinges. Two stone eagles guarded the entrance, angry wings outstretched.

"A fitting description, don't you think, for the days in which this house was built?" he grinned, his glance going upwards, then led her into the big, shadowy hall with its wide fire-place that looked as if it could roast an ox and in days gone by, probably had.

There was a scraping of chairs and a voice came from a room to the left.

"I wonder if we'll hear today when

our guest is to arrive. I suppose she'll land up on the doorstep without even so much as a warning to say that she is coming. Young people are so thoughtless these days."

The words had been uttered by a woman and had held more than a hint of malice.

"And I suppose she'll expect to be waited on hand and foot. Plenty of servants in Singapore, so I've been told." This from a man. "*Maman*, don't let her sponge on you, whatever happens. I know that soft heart of yours."

Beth turned to Gawen, indignant colour burning her tanned cheeks, but before she could say anything another voice chimed in.

"I think you're both absolutely horrid. Ruan, I've never known you to prejudge before."

The outburst lifted Gawen's mouth into a quirk of amusement. He gave her an encouraging push.

"That's *Maman* standing up for you.

We'd better stop eaves-dropping."

There was a sudden silence from the room as Beth's high heeled shoes tapped across the polished floor.

"Here's our visitor," said Gawen cheerfully, enjoying his family's discomforture.

"Beth!" cried her godmother, coming forward eagerly. She looked like some small bird whose feathers had just been badly ruffled.

Beth found her hands taken in a warm clasp and was pulled down to meet her diminutive godmother's lips.

"Dear child! How nice to see you again, but what an awful day to choose. Come and meet the rest of my family."

Mrs. Trevelgen had a mass of silvery hair and a soft, delicate complexion, her hazel eyes kind, but Beth's impression of Sophia, Gawen's wife, was not so flattering.

She was a youngish woman in her early thirties, tall, well-built in a tweed skirt and matching twinset in a heather mixture of greens and browns. Dark hair and eyes that did not even try to hide their hostility.

Beth's own eyes were still stormy as her godmother turned to introduce her eldest son.

So this was the Master of Truran. A face carved in granite with hair the colour of a raven's wing, springing from a wide brow. He had a similar build to that of his brother, but his uncommunicative eyes were a deeper blue.

So here was another who was unprepared to welcome her, Beth thought wryly and then her head came up proudly, eyes as cool as his. She had no intention of letting him see how he had ruffled her. In her profession there had been ample scope for handling difficult patients and she would treat him as such.

"I couldn't help overhear your remarks, Mr. Trevelgen. If it will put your mind at rest, I'm leaving again tomorrow night and as to your other accusation — yes, you were quite right. I've always been surrounded by servants, but let me tell you this, if we hadn't employed these people, they could well have been amongst the thousands of unfortunate unemployed living in the shanty towns around Singapore, not knowing where their next meal will come from. It's as basic as that." She went on levelly. "Now my old nurse and the gardener will be able to live in comfort for the rest of their lives on the money they were able to save."

Beth became conscious of the stares of the rest of the family. A defiant note crept into her voice.

"I'm quite capable of making my own bed and *amah* saw to it that Fenella and I were taught to cook and sew."

Ruan's dark glance swept over her, taking in the minutest detail, or so Beth felt and if she had expected an apology, she was disappointed for all he said was:

"Good, now perhaps we'll have a

change of menu. Chinese food is quite a favourite with me," with that maddening smile of his.

"What a shame you'll be leaving us so soon," cut in Gawen still with that unholy look of amusement, as he lounged in a chair, one leg crossed comfortably over the other, quite prepared to spend the entire morning there. "You won't be able to meet our spook then."

"Don't talk nonsense," his brother said sharply, frowning as if some memory had troubled him. "Come along, we can't waste all day." His voice was deep with only a faint trace of Cornish accent and as he bent to kiss his mother's soft cheek, Beth frowned.

Where had she seen this man before?

2

MRS. TREVELGEN drew Beth's arm through hers as they mounted the old oak staircase with its worn red carpet, her hazel eyes mischievous.

"My dear, you're like a refreshing breeze on a hot summer's day. I'm glad you stood up to that very rude son of mine but I do hope you'll make allowances for him. He's an embittered man these days, if that is any excuse for bad manners." She broke off with a sigh and a sideways glance at the girl beside her.

What lovely colouring this god-daughter of hers had, thought Mrs. Trevelgen with affection and how well that sherry silk skin and wide grey eyes toned in with that cap of copper velvet.

They were crossing the spacious

gallery now, high, with dark oak beams against a white-washed ceiling, wrought iron brackets holding all lights.

Beth's shoes tapped hollowly as they entered the short passage in the West wing. No carpets here, she noticed. In fact, the whole house had a faded air of past glories, gone for ever.

"We thought this room would be nice for you, dear child. I'm across there," with a nod at two doors on the opposite wall. "I hope you'll be comfortable in here."

"I'm sure I will, Aunt May. There is a wonderful feeling of being back in the past of smugglers and wreckers which intrigues me. I suppose it must be because this house is so old. The one we had in Singapore was modern in every respect and a little impersonal."

Beth glanced around her, eyes joyous, but turned with surprise when Mrs. Trevelgen said with a note of asperity:

"We've always been a most respectable family."

Beth's mouth twitched. Her god-mother was arranging the chintz curtains as if their folds did not quite suit her neat taste, dignity in every line of the small body.

"I think this is a lovely room, Aunt May," Beth hastened to add.

"Beth, you are to forget everything while you are here with us. Time enough to worry when you have to. There are lines on your face, dear child, that shouldn't be there at your age and you are much too thin," with a disapproving nod at the slim figure in the well-fitting leaf-green dress.

She drew Beth down, cupping her face between her small hands and kissed her on both cheeks and Beth remembered that this family had French roots deep in the past.

"I'll leave you to do your unpacking. Come along to my room when you are ready and we'll have a nice long chat."

The door closed behind her godmother and Beth was left with her thoughts.

Yes, she would forget her worries for thirty-six hours. She stretched her arms high above her head, and turned to the window.

The roar of the waves could be plainly heard as they crashed on to the boulders below. There was a sheer drop on this side of the house and a little out to sea, rose a stark towering column of rock, a home for birds and a sentinel guarding Truran House. What a landmark it must have made for smugglers!

Her thoughts turned to the man who owned all this. How arrogantly he had looked down his long, aquiline nose at her this morning, his dark blue eyes hard in a face made brown from the elements of his native Cornwall. Square cut chin and straight, disapproving lips had bade her no welcome and yet, she found she had to admire that firm jut of his jaw, for here was no pale imitation of a man and went on to wonder what had made him as he was. A woman perhaps? It couldn't

35

possibly be anything else, for wasn't he Master of Truran, by the stroke of one hour? Gawen should be the embittered one, but he seemed the most affable of men, but what about Sophia, his wife? Here was someone quite different. Hard and ambitious, was the way Beth read her.

She turned away from the window and started to unpack. These people's lives did not really concern her, for by tomorrow night she would have gone, but she did just wonder.

"Your sons are so different Aunt May. One would never dream they are twins."

They were seated in Mrs. Trevelgen's small sittingroom, Beth kneeling on the wide window seat, enjoying the sparkle of sunlight on water and the ragged sweep of the headland.

"No," agreed Aunt May. "Ruan is a strong, dependable person and I don't know what I would have done without him when my husband died, but he is a little difficult, even though I shouldn't say it." She smiled reminiscently. "As the boys grew up, the villagers used to say that it wasn't surprising Ruan fought his way into the world first for even as a very small boy, he was the leader and Gawen quite content to let it be so, but he pulls his weight in our pottery business."

"Do you mine china clay here?" Beth's glance had come around with interest.

"No, this is not the area for it, but we make handmade pottery and find the tourists like our novelties. Gawen is extremely artistic and does all the designing of shape and decoration."

A rueful expression chased across Mrs. Trevelgen's face.

"I wish sometimes he would exert himself more. He's quite happy to let Sophia run his life. Perhaps I'm old fashioned."

"It says a lot for his happy nature though, that he has never developed an inferiority complex with having a brother like Ruan," said Beth.

37

"Yes, he's an uncomplicated soul and now, dear child, that's enough about my family. What's all this nonsense about staying only one night? I expected to have you here for at least a month." Mrs. Trevelgen was regarding her with a frown between her delicately arched brows, the hazel eyes reproachful.

Beth's glance was affectionate as it rested on her diminutive godmother.

"It's sweet of you. Thank you, but I can't possibly do that. You have your family — " How could she explain that she could never feel free to accept her godmother's hospitality, not in the face of Ruan's and Sophia's unfriendliness.

"Aunt May, I'm twenty-three and then there is Fenella, I must give her a home."

"Ah yes, poor Fenella," murmured her godmother with deep compassion.

"I got to know that child very well over the years and what she always longed for, was her parents love. My heart has often ached for you two girls."

Beth was startled.

"But we were a very united family."

"In the holidays, perhaps."

"What on earth are you trying to say, Aunt May?"

"You were both sent away to school to New Zealand at such a tender age and that doesn't strike me as being a particularly united family."

"But most of the white population sent their children away to school. Singapore is not a healthy climate," Beth protested, "and Fen has always been considered delicate and besides, it was Fen's own wish that she be sent over here to school, then do a year in Switzerland."

"It seemed that Marta and Bill used to chase off in that yacht of theirs as soon as you two had been packed off to school," she said tartly.

"But we had lovely holidays." Perplexity had deepened Beth's voice and the grey in her thickly lashed eyes. "Singapore and the islands around about have wonderful beaches and we used to go for picnics — oh, there was heaps to do. What yarn has Fen been spinning you, Aunt May?" she asked indignantly.

"Only that she felt that her parents never loved her sufficiently. She hated being sent away to school."

"I know she didn't like the discipline, but it is quite untrue that Mum and Dad did not love her. As for neglecting us that's not true," she said fiercely.

"There, dear, I'm sorry. I've made you really angry," smiling a little at the stormy rain-clear grey eyes.

"But did you never feel left out, like Fen did?" Mrs. Trevelgen asked curiously.

"No, never," Beth said vehemently. "It looks as if I don't know my sister at all."

Her hands clenched again in her lap. She had never even had an inkling of the uncertainties and heartache that must have pulled Fenella to pieces all these years, or had the little minx been angling for a large dose of sympathy?

Beth turned to the window again to hide the shadow of pain in her eyes. Far below the sea washed the age-old coastline with foaming lace, the sky above, a brilliant blue.

Mrs. Trevelgen had risen, her hand pressing warm against Beth's shoulder. "I'm sure things will work out," she said gently. "I wanted you to know what to expect when you meet Fen again. I'm afraid you have a difficult passage in front of you, Beth, for you have painted such a different picture. I'm quite annoyed with Fen for all the tarradiddles she has told." The finely etched brows came down sharply over the hazel eyes in a frown, but cleared as she looked at her god-daughter. "Now, dear child, I really must go and help Sophia. Would you like to wander outside until lunch time? It's turned out to be a lovely day."

"Isn't there anything I can do to help?" Beth asked swiftly, Ruan's harsh accusations coming to her again.

Mrs. Trevelgen shook her snowy

white head firmly.

"No, you go and get a breath of fresh air."

Beth entered the hall again an hour later, satiated with the magnificence of the view from the terrace of sea, cliffs, village and headland and in a much calmer frame of mind. It was warm and cosy in the huge hall, the chimney-place blackened with countless fires, had a fine copper screen hiding its gaping mouth.

Ruan came in and offered her a sherry.

"How can you be so different from Fenella?" he demanded. "Fen's like spindrift," an indulgent note in his deep voice.

Beth was very conscious of his controlled strength and width of shoulder as he handed her a glass.

"And I suppose I'm a bit more substantial," she could not help retorting tartly. "I took after my father," unease again troubling the grey eyes, but surely Fenella, at eighteen would not be the unsettled child who had left home three years previously, or even the person who had gone to the Continent a year ago?

"Fen must have taken after your mother, then," his glance going to the shaft of sunlight burnishing her hair to a soft copper glow.

Ruan had perched himself against the window frame, his long legs stretched out before him, one hand in pocket, the other holding his glass.

"Those cool grey eyes of yours belie that tawny topknot, if I'm not mistaken. I'm wondering what the real Beth is like," one eyebrow raised, dark blue eyes amused.

"You won't be able to find out, will you?"

A young girl began laying the table in the diningroom.

"I see you also keep servants, Mr. Trevelgen."

If Beth had hoped to put him out of countenance, she was disappointed, for he merely smiled aggravatingly.

"You angling for an apology?"

"It would be polite, now wouldn't it? One would have thought that you did not employ servants, the way that snide remark of yours came out this morning."

"Lunch is ready."

They both turned as an elderly woman appeared in the doorway, regarding Beth curiously.

"Not another one," Beth murmured, as they rose to their feet.

Ruan signalled with an exaggerated gesture of the hand for her to precede him.

"After you, Miss Dexter," an answering gleam, a devil dancing in the dark depths of his eyes.

The appetising smell of cheese souffle, made Beth suddenly conscious that she was ravenously hungry. Breakfast had been served on the train at a very early hour and that seemed ages ago.

"Maggie, this is my godchild," said Mrs. Trevelgen to the old woman who had called them in to lunch. "Beth, this is Maggie, who has been with me for more years than I care to count and who is as dear to me as my right hand."

"Please to meet you, Miss," the dumpy body bobbing.

Maggie was bent with rheumatism, with a face pouched and puckered with age and yet out of that face peeped the brightest eyes Beth had ever seen. They were twinkling now with pleasure and curiosity.

"And a very nice young lady too," said Maggie back in her kitchen, nodding her approval at the black cat curled up in a chair next to the old fashioned coal stove.

Sophia, who had been reading a letter when Beth came into the room, folded its pages, her austere face glowing with happy pride.

"Denzel won't be coming home for Easter," she said to her mother-in-law. "He's going to a scout camp."

"Denzel is eight," explained Mrs.

45

Trevelgen to Beth. "A dear dear little fellow."

"A little devil, you mean," growled Ruan.

"How can you say that about your heir?" fired up Sophia, her dark eyes angry. She had quite failed to catch the affectionate note that had edged Ruan's words.

Beth's puzzled frown met her godmother's suddenly wary glance. How could Sophia possibly talk of her son being heir to Truran? After all, Ruan was only a little over thirty and was more than likely to marry himself one day. This reluctant host of hers was beginning to make her curious.

That afternoon Mrs. Trevelgen and Beth set out for a drive with Gawen at the wheel. Soon they were travelling along incredibly narrow lanes, the hedgerows a blaze of colour. Honeysuckle, fuchsias, foxgloves and marguerites, mingled harmoniously with bracken and fern.

"Spring comes early to Cornwall," said her godmother, pleased at Beth's gasp of delight at the sight of a field of tulips and anemones, workers moving swiftly down the rows, fingers deft and quick.

"Those blooms will be sent on the night train to London and people will be able to buy them tomorrow morning on their way to work."

Gawen stopped at an old Inn and suggested tea.

"Aunt May, wouldn't you rather go back home?" asked Beth, her glance keen and professional. Her godmother looked far from well.

"I'm all right, dear. A cup of tea would be nice."

Mrs. Trevelgen came into Beth's room while she was dressing for dinner that evening, resplendent in a black lace frock of ancient design and a large, old-fashioned diamond brooch at her throat.

"Oh, am I late?" asked Beth, hurriedly glancing down at her watch.

"No, dear child. I'm early," sinking down into a chair with obvious effort.

"Aunt May, don't you think you should be in bed?"

"Please don't fuss." The tone was impatient. "Now what was I wanting to say to you? Oh dear, it's quite gone." A fragile hand was passed across her eyes, with evident distress.

Beth watched her with growing anxiety; the pinched mouth and the too pale cheeks.

"Don't worry, Aunt May. It will come, but there is something I'm dying to ask you. I was surprised at lunch when Sophia talked about Denzel being Ruan's heir."

A hint of sadness feathered over Mrs. Trevelgen's face and she moved restlessly in her chair.

"Yes, I could see you were."

Beth turned around again on the tapestry stool.

"It's true then what Sophia said, but how old is Ruan? Thirty, thirty-one?" Her godmother nodded. "Surely he'll marry one of these days? It — it's such a strange arrangement."

48

"I don't think Ruan will ever marry, Beth," her godmother said sadly. "He was engaged to a girl long ago, but she was tragically killed in a car accident on the eve of their wedding and I've watched my son, over the years, grow from a gentle, lovable person into a taciturn, embittered man."

"But sorrow is surely obliterated by time?" objected Beth. There was something here she could not understand.

"Ah, but what of bitterness? That is not so easily wiped out." She paused to stare blindly into the fire. "When Laylia died, he made a will in Denzel's favour." The delicate veined lids hid the hazel eyes and there was no expression in her next words. "Sophia was delighted."

Beth had a sudden impish wish that Ruan would marry. It would serve this scheming woman right to have all her precious ambitions overset.

They had not been seated long in the oak panelled hall, when Ruan came down the stairs, every muscle beautifully co-ordinated in that well-knit frame. Gawen and Sophia followed soon after and the family went in to dinner.

"Come through into the lounge, Beth," said Mrs. Trevelgen when the meal ended. "Maggie will have taken the coffee in there."

Beth sat close to the fire, savouring its welcome warmth. Living in the Far East had not conditioned her for this cold, but she joined Gawen at the window when he beckoned her over, the fragrance of freshly made coffee a beneficence after a very well cooked meal.

"What do you think of our eerie?" he asked.

"It's beautiful," awe in her voice. The coastline stretched out before her, the westering sun softly gilding its ragged lines with liquid fire, the last dying embers tipped out rosy-red on cliff and sea alike.

"Yes," agreed Gawen, but his eyes were on the silky hair and the tanned curve of her cheek.

"Wait until the winter winds shriek around the house like a legion of banshees and the days have none of the magic you see now," put in Ruan unkindly. "You'll change your mind then."

There was a hawklike quality about him this evening that made Beth long to be away from here.

"Dear child, I'd love you to consider this your home now," said Mrs. Trevelgen eagerly, "and don't let Ruan put you off."

Her son stiffened.

"Perhaps Miss Dexter has other plans, *Maman*." His tone was the jab of a goad. "After all, an out of the way place on the Cornish coast, might not be all to her liking."

"Oh, snap out of it, Ruan," chuckled Gawen, hunching himself even further into his dinner jacket. "It will do you all the good in the world to have a lovely lady under your highbred nose for once. Dash it all, it's not natural the way you shun all feminine society. Just give me the chance — " He stopped as he caught his wife's warning eye.

Ruan's whole manner had changed. The mocking smile had gone and in its place, cold anger and a sweep of contempt, his blue eyes slits under the well formed brows.

He had risen and Beth watched him put his cup on the trolley.

"I must get those plans drawn up. Lomas is coming tomorrow, so if you'll excuse me — "

"Ruan!"

His mother's voice made him turn at the door and glance over his shoulder.

"Can't they wait just one evening? Beth goes tomorrow."

His eyebrows arched, the dark eyes going to the girl framed in the window, her tawny head aglow.

"*Maman*, I'm sure Miss Dexter will be far more comfortable without my presence, attractive picture though she may make. It's wonderful how women live for effect."

He was gone, the room strangely empty. Beth frowned.

"Well, I don't like you either, Mr. Trevelgen," and found Gawen's amused gaze fixed on her.

Her godmother gave an exasperated sigh, tapping one small hand on the chair arm.

"Do you really mean to leave us tomorrow evening, Miss Dexter?" asked Sophia with a hard black stare. "Or have you changed your mind?" registering a resentment she did not even try to hide, her knitting stilled, hands clenched tight around the needles.

Beth nodded and was not surprised when relief washed the tension from the elder woman's face and she began knitting again.

"Tell us about Singapore, Beth," said Gawen lazily. "I'm interested in the Far East, especially their art."

"From an armchair, you mean," snapped his wife. "You would be much too indolent to make the effort to go there."

"Just give me the money, my girl and then watch me," he retorted amicably.

Mrs. Trevelgen rose from her chair and Beth sprang to help her. "You're not starting on Singapore tonight. This child has had a tiring day and we're both going to bed."

Even though it had been a long day, Beth did not immediately go to bed. The sound of crashing waves drew her to the window. For a long time she gazed out at the night-filled sky, the stars, precious gems on a velvet cushion, her thoughts winging nostalgically back to Singapore and Kim. What was he doing at this moment and knew a moment of panic, with not the slightest idea as to what time it was over there.

"Oh Kim! Come soon," she whispered with longing, memory a lingering ache behind her closed lids.

Beth woke slowly the next morning and for a moment did not know where she was, then it all came to her. This was Truran House.

She threw back the bed clothes and pattered to the window. The blue of the sea called her, the sands golden in the sun, the weired, wild cries of the gulls, a familiar sound in unfamiliar surroundings. She quickly took out her swim-suit and put it on, gave her hair a superficial brushing, grabbed her towel, then hurried out of the house.

For a moment Beth leant contentedly against the stone parapet, cold against her skin and gazed her fill at the sea frothing on the sands of the cove, scalloped out of the rocks. A flight of stone steps, cut in a cleft in the cliff, invited her on to the beach.

She dived in quickly, the water icy. Here was no tropical sea and swam for a little longer, but the cold in her body decided her that it was time to get out. To her horror, cramp seized her feet in such a vice-like grip that she began to flounder, knew a moment of panic and turned over on her back, but the pain was excruciating. Beth turned over again, the water closing over her head and didn't even realize she had called for help.

"All right," a voice rapped out close to her ear and felt a hard hand grip her shoulder.

Beth couldn't stop the instinctive urge to grab at Ruan, her heart pounding chokingly in her throat, blanking out all sound and sight.

"Don't do that," he said furiously. "Do you want us both to drown?"

He had her under the armpits now and was slowly pulling her in. Beth willed herself to keep still, the waves breaking over her upturned face with merciless force, then, after what seemed an age, felt the coarse sand under her back, rasping at her skin and found herself once more on the beach, gasping for breath, very much like a fish that had just been landed.

"My feet," struggling to sit up, the words coming through lips that had gone blue.

"Here, let me massage them for you," said Ruan, placing her towel

56

and his over her shoulders. The pain made her bite back a cry, her toes continuing to curl under.

"Stretch your feet and pull them upwards as far as they will go and keep them like that," he ordered.

Slowly the pain receded, leaving Beth limp and exhausted and she tentatively relaxed her muscles, but the cramp seized her again and a cry escaped her.

"Hang on for a bit," Ruan said authoritatively. He was still massaging her feet that were taking on a pinkish tinge. His dark hair lay straight over his forehead and Beth was acutely aware of the broad shoulders as he bent over her, the well developed muscles rippling under the tanned skin.

At last Beth was able to stand up.

"Thank goodness you were there," she said with a shudder.

Ruan pushed the heavy fall of hair impatiently from off his forehead.

"Thought something like this might happen. That's why I came down."

"How very gratifying for you to have your prediction proved correct," she said sarcastically, finding her wits still active even though her body was shivering violently.

"Run," ordered Ruan, bundling her unceremoniously along. "Why on earth you decided to have a dip so early in the year, beats me. You should have known it would be too cold." He began hauling her up the long flight of stone steps.

"I like swimming." Her chin came up defiantly at him.

Beth was gasping for breath by the time they were half way up the steps, the relentless hand gripping hers, showing no mercy.

"Don't go so fast," she had to plead at last.

The grey stone house still seemed no nearer, solid and almost forbidding on the top of the cliff.

Ruan's glance flashed down at her.

"Do you want a chill? What you need right now is a hot bath and some breakfast inside of you."

Beth shot a look of dislike at his broad back and said tauntingly:

"Afraid I'll not be able to leave tonight, Mr. Trevelgen?"

They had at last reached the terrace, Beth trying to get her breath back, her body gloriously warm.

"If I'm not mistaken, you're tough," he said opening the door for her. "We'll go up the back stairs. It's the quickest."

"Thank you for rescuing me," she said gruffly, her clear grey eyes meeting his, her hair already fluff-dry at the ends.

His wide shoulders lifted in a shrug, his glance darkly mocking.

"One can't allow even an enemy to drown."

Beth was startled at the harsh words. So she was to be the scapegoat for the hurt dealt out to him by the hand of fate so long ago.

"I take it from that, you don't like my sex, Mr. Trevelgen?"

"Any reason why I should?" His lean face had hardened, memory ridden. "I have yet to find loyalty in women."

"But, Aunt May — " clutching the towel more closely around her, as they traversed the wide passage, grey eyes indignant.

"I'm not discussing my mother," his voice dry. "She belongs to another generation, another age."

Was he generalizing then, or had the girl he was to have married, played him false? It could account for the bitterness in him. She tilted her head to look up at him.

"I can only presume you must be judging on one instance only and I'm sorry for you. How can you be so narrow minded as to condemn all women for the sins of one?" Her grey eyes were pitying.

The lean profile had hardened and she knew she had been correct in her surmise.

"You had better go and have a bath," Ruan said tight-lipped, before disappearing into his room.

Mrs. Trevelgen did not come down to breakfast that morning and when Beth went to see her, found her lying amongst her pillows, quite talkative, but the delicately traced features were tired.

"I sometimes have a morning in bed," said her godmother in answer to Beth's anxious query. "Now, don't worry, dear child. It is just old age catching up with me."

Beth looked at her godmother affectionately.

"Dear Aunt May."

"You know, dear child, I'm not happy about you going away tonight," said Mrs. Trevelgen, a look of doubt troubling her face. "You are quite peeky."

Beth chuckled.

"Talk about me being peeky. What about you?" and went on to tell her godmother how Ruan had rescued her. "I got the fright of my life. The awful feel of water closing over my head and not able to do a thing about it and that terrible cramp." She shivered at the recollection.

Mrs. Trevelgen had gone white and clutched at Beth's hands as she sat on the edge of the bed.

"That settles it. You are not to go tonight. What a blessing Ruan was there."

Beth leant forward and kissed the soft cheek nearest to her.

"I must go, Aunt May. Please don't stop me," she pleaded.

"Very well, dear. I can't stop you, if that is the way you really feel," still unconvinced.

Ruan was to drive Beth to the station.

"You'll write and tell us how you get on, won't you?" said Mrs. Trevelgen, as Beth bent to kiss her.

"I'll go one better, Aunt May, you'll be asked to stay, just as soon as I've been able to get a flat."

Beth got into the car after having said goodbye to Sophia and Gawen, and Ruan shut the door.

He drove inland, leaving the jagged, pinnacled coastline, that reminded Beth of savage black teeth against the purple-grey sky and marvelled again at the ever changing face of Cornwall.

She stole a glance at her companion's uncompromising nose and chin etched sharply against the fast moving country-side and tried desperately to think of something to say, but there was nothing. She could not even say she was sorry to be leaving Truran House.

The train was already in the station by the time they arrived and Beth was soon settled in her compartment. Ruan said goodbye and she watched him stride out of the exit, without even so much as a backward glance on his part.

Ruan drove back home. A faint, very feminine perfume still lingered in the car, making him believe she was still there beside him, a slim girl with capable hands and cool grey eyes and that hair — . He could still see its amber softness.

He wound down the window with an impatient twist. Just as well she had gone for he would never allow another woman to intrude into his life again after what Laylia had done to him and yet he could not still his thoughts. That blue outfit had suited her somehow, the pill-box hat sitting so demurely at the back of her head.

An hour later the train stopped at yet another station, but Beth was so immersed in her thoughts, that for a moment, when she heard her name being called, the fact did not register immediately.

"Miss Dexter? Miss Beth Dexter?" The ticket examiner was consulting his list of passengers.

"Yes," hurriedly excusing herself to her fellow travellers and popping her head out of the window.

The Station Master had come up now, stout, his red face perspiring heavily.

"Sorry, Miss," he said apologetically,

"but would you please leave the train. I have an urgent message from a Mr. Trevelgen of Truran."

"Hope it isn't bad news, dearie," said a motherly woman, while a dapper little man with a military moustache took down Beth's case.

She smiled a little uncertainly at them all, before hurrying along the corridor.

The Station Master helped her alight and took her along the platform, the interested and curious eyes of a whole carriageful of passengers following them. A whistle was blown, a green flag fluttered and the train pulled out of the station.

"What is this all about and what is the message?" asked Beth, her fingers tense on her handbag, grey eyes dark with apprehension.

"Come into my office, Miss." The plump little man pulled out a chair for her, then seated himself opposite. He put on his glasses and peered at the note he had on his pad. "Like I said,

Miss, this Mr. Trevelgen asked me, by phone, to get you off that train. Said it was urgent."

"But why?" asked Beth impatiently.

"Well, it says here to tell you that his mother has been taken ill." He pulled off his glasses and fiddled with them nervously. "It's all highly irregular, Miss. You do know that, don't you? Do you know Mr. Trevelgen?" Small, black eyes were suddenly suspicious under those thick, wildly untidy brows.

Beth nodded mutely. Her godmother had been perfectly all right when she had left her, not two hours ago.

"Did — did Mr. Trevelgen say how bad his mother was?" she faltered.

"No, Miss, but if you don't want to go back there for any reason, you just say the word and I'll find a way out for you. As I have said before, this is all highly irregular." Officialdom had once more taken over, making the waistcoated chest swell visibly.

"Not running away, are you?" he leered jokingly.

Beth gave a little laugh and pulled herself together. Her apprehension must have been mirrored on her face, for here was this absurd man thinking all manner of things. It was evident he was an ardent TV fan.

"It's all perfectly simple," she hastened to assure him. "Mrs. Trevelgen is my godmother and I've been staying with her for a few days. I'm sorry she's been taken ill."

"You just sit there, Miss, and make yourself comfortable. No doubt Mr. Trevelgen will be along presently to collect you."

3

RUAN found Beth half an hour later, still seated in the Station Master's dingy office. He appeared enormous, in the doorway of the small room, black hair shining from the light shed by two bulbs suspended from the high ceiling.

She quickly rose to her feet, wide grey eyes anxiously searching his.

"What happened and how is Aunt May?"

"*Maman* had a nasty fall just after you left. Whether that caused the slight heart attack or the heart attack caused the fall, we aren't certain. The doctor suggested hospital, but *Maman* wouldn't hear of it. That is why I got you off the train."

There was not a smidgen of apology in his dark eyes, or even a polite enquiry as to whether she was willing to go back with him. Only a cold arrogance that made her curl her fingers tight against her palms.

"I'm so sorry," she murmured. "I'll most certainly stay until a nurse can be found, but," tilting her chin defiantly at him, "I hope you realise, Mr. Trevelgen, I'm only doing this for Godmother."

Ruan's straight brows rose in a cynical curve.

"You'll stay as long as my mother needs you," his voice cut in hard and inflexible, his hand shooting out, his fingers pitiless on her wrist.

Beth's face was stormy as she faced him.

"I do not really wish to go back to Truran House."

"Well, don't let *Maman* guess that," he said tight-lipped. "I had the impression you would have jumped at the chance of doing something for her, but I see I was mistaken."

Beth struggled to break from those hurting fingers.

69

"You know I'd do anything for Aunt May!" Her voice shook with indignation at the condemnation on his face that was as hard as the grip on her wrist. "You don't want me back at Truran House either, Mr. Trevelgen. You are doing this very much against your will."

"I'll put up with you for *Maman*'s sake. Treat this as another job, if it will make you feel any happier."

Beth stared at him, speechless. A head shorter than he was, put her at an immediate disadvantage.

"Both you and Sophia made it abundantly clear that I was very much of an unwelcome guest."

"Come on, we're wasting precious time talking here," taking her impatiently by the arm. "We can argue it out in the car."

"You'd better tell that little Station Master I'm going willingly," a gleam of mischief trembling her mouth as she tried to keep up with his long strides. "He's sure I'm being forcibly abducted, or something equally as silly."

Ruan stopped short with a ludicrous expression chasing over his features.

"Oh Lord!" The exclamation broke from him boyishly. "I wonder what wild stories he'll circulate among his cronies tonight. I'd better go and sort him out."

"One more story won't harm you, will it?" she asked sweetly.

With an exasperated shrug Ruan strode off, but was soon back.

Rebellion suddenly pushed out her anxiety for her godmother. Beth did not want to go back to Truran House. There was no consideration for anyone in this man. He was as feudal as that bleak house of his, perched in proud isolation on its promontory.

"And what about Fenella?" Beth demanded as they went down the station steps. She had forgotten all about her sister.

"Fen can come down here if you haven't left by the time she finishes school," he threw at her over his shoulder.

"Of course, flats and jobs are so easily found these days in London," she couldn't help retorting shrewishly.

"I'll come up to town with you and sort things out," his tone one of nicely calculated sarcasm.

Beth was silenced. It was the last thing she wanted — to be in this man's debt.

Ruan started up the car and backed it expertly out of the station yard.

"I've practically no clothes," she said in a small voice, when they had left the small town behind. "My two trunks are at Euston."

"I'll get them down to you," he said evenly.

They drove back along the rain-drenched lanes in a hostile silence, the green of leaf and grass brilliantly accentuated by moisture and headlights.

Truran Village loomed ahead of them an hour later.

Ruan glanced across at her, sitting stiff against her corner, noticing the sensitive, rebellious curve of her mouth.

"So, you're still sore at me," he observed mildly. "I'm sorry, I know I do tend to ride roughshod over people." His voice was as near as it would ever get to being an apology and then he startled Beth still further by stopping the car and saying carefully: "Would you like me to take you back to the station? There is a later train you could catch. Just say the word."

For the second time that evening, Beth found no words with which to answer him. He had taken her completely by surprise. She could not see his face properly, the shadows blurring that strong outline of nose and jaw, but there was no doubting the sincerity of the next words.

"We really do need you, Beth."

Beth was instantly mollified and smiled at him in her friendly way.

"Why didn't you say that long ago?" she said swiftly. "I might have been a bit more amenable. I never did like being press-ganged into anything."

Ruan started up the car.

"Thank you, Beth."

The light had gone now, the headlights picking up weird shapes at the side of the road.

Expediency had momentarily cracked this man's hard reserve, and Beth was under no illusion that it would soften permanently. He needed her help badly and was willing to tolerate her for his mother's sake. Well, she could at least do the same.

"Is Aunt May very bad?"

Ruan changed gear as they went through the massive gates of Truran House, which stood shadowy and unreal against the darkening skyline and Beth shivered. All the curtains must be drawn for no welcoming light showed.

"Old Doctor Jenkins holds out every hope for her recovery, but she'll need careful nursing during the next couple of weeks or so, which I'm sure you'll be able to give her, Beth."

Ruan took Beth up the wide branched staircase that rose from the hall below, along the gallery with its numerous family portraits of the Masters of Truran. The doctor was sitting near the bed, but rose when they entered. Sophia was also there, standing well back in the shadows, her face expressionless. Beth looked beyond the doctor and caught her breath in swift pity and crossed to her godmother's side. White and frail, she lay there, with deep sunk eyes and Beth was suddenly afraid. She had nursed for years, always experiencing a deep pity when disaster had come to others, but this was different. Here was someone she loved and all she could do was stand and suffer too. This dear person must not die. Aunt May was her only link with the past, apart from Fenella, and felt that something precious given to her yesterday could well be snatched from her today.

Beth held the small hand in hers and a thin wavering smile, soon gone, told her that her godmother was conscious of her presence.

Tears threatened to close Beth's

throat, used as she was to illness, the still figure in the big bed moved her uncontrollably.

It was the doctor who recalled her.

"I'm very pleased to have you here, Miss Dexter," he said, ushering her out into the passage. "Mrs. Trevelgen will need expert attention and I'm glad she'll have a nurse she knows." The alert brown eyes below fly-away brows beetled over Beth. "Call me immediately you think there is any change for the worse," and then went on to give her instructions for the rest of the night.

They had crossed the gallery and were standing at the top of the stairs, the rotund doctor only coming to Beth's shoulder.

"There is no need to see me down, Sister. I've been coming to this house for years. Ah, I see Gawen in the hall. He'll see me out and is no doubt waiting anxiously for a report on his mother. Goodnight."

Beth returned to her Aunt's room.

Sophia had gone, but Ruan was still there, the shaded lamp trowelling dark shadows on his taut face. He held out his hand and Beth put hers into it with a look of enquiry in the clear grey eyes.

"Thank you," he said again, his other hand going out in a curiously defenceless gesture and then he was gone.

Beth went across to the bed and saw that her godmother's eyes were open, hazed with the drug the doctor had administered earlier that evening. She gave a little cry of welcome but her smile was a pathetic grimace.

Beth firmed her lips to stop them trembling and managed to say:

"Fancy doing a thing like this the minute my back was turned," her fingers on the too rapid pulse.

"I did think your stay was too short, dear child," came the indomitable reply. "So pleased to see you. You're not to worry about Fenella, or that job or a flat — " The words came out in a slurred whisper, the fragile hands clutching with frenzied strength, but the effort was too much and they dropped again to the coverlet. "You'll stay?"

Beth bent to kiss the parchment forehead that was far too hot and dry.

"I'll stay as long as you need me, Aunt May," and had the satisfaction of seeing her godmother relax among the piled up pillows, eyes closed again.

Towards morning Mrs. Trevelgen stirred again.

"Beth?" The word was no more than a sigh.

"I'm here, Aunt May." Beth quietly moved to the bed and gently imprisoned the wandering hands. "Can I get you something?"

"I thought I'd dreamed you had come back. Don't let them take me to hospital, Beth — please." The hazel eyes were eloquent in their pleading, the breath coming through the trembling lips, laboured and painful.

"I promise I'll stay here, Aunt May," was all Beth vouchsafed. "Now don't worry," gently tucking in a wisp of grey hair that had fallen over the veined forehead. "I'm going to raise you higher. It will help your breathing."

Beth held her godmother up with one arm and began to plump up the pillows and found Ruan beside her.

"I'll hold her while you do that." Very gently he took his mother's weight. "You're doing fine, *Maman*. We'll soon have you on those two small feet again. You know how we need you downstairs to keep the peace."

Beth was amazed at his gentleness. She had begun to wonder if there could possibly be any of the softer emotions in that granite interior of his.

"She seems very restless. How long before the next injection?" asked Ruan in a low tone away from the bed.

Beth looked at her watch.

"Not for another hour, I'm afraid."

He went back to the bed and laid a hand over the troubled one. Mrs.

Trevelgen opened her eyes and a pleased gleam lightened her face as she looked at them both.

"I'm so glad you've made up your difference at last," she whispered. "You won't ever be lonely again, Ruan."

He was startled.

"She thinks we're married."

Beth nodded. She knew very sick people often did have strange flights of fancy.

The whispered words went on.

"Beth will make you a lovely wife."

"I'm sure she will, *Mamam*," he replied softly. "Now go to sleep. It will give you the healing you need."

How often Beth had seen the touch of a loved one soothe a patient and saw it happen now. She slipped out of the room, returning with two cups of hot coffee and a plate of sandwiches. Ruan looked up in acknowledgment as she placed them by his side.

Her godmother was asleep, the fingers of dawn, intensifying into day, picking out clearly the old-fashioned furniture and rose-strewn walls.

Maggie came into the room just after eight.

"You're to go down to breakfast. I'll watch the Mistress for a wee while. How is she?" The usually twinkling eyes were anxious.

"I think there is an improvement."

"Praise be for that," came the fervent reply. "I'm very pleased to see you back, Miss Beth. We need you here. That one," with a contemptuous nod over her shoulder in the direction of the East Wing, "has no sense at all when it comes to nursing. Unwomanly I calls it and yet give her something to do with business — " She shrugged the rheumaticky, bent shoulders under the black knitted shawl, edging a little closer to Beth. "And what is more, she didn't want you called back. Master Ruan might lose his heart to you and that wouldn't suit my lady's book at all."

Sophia came up the stairs.

"All right, Maggie," she snapped.

"This is no time for a gossip. I wondered why Miss Dexter had not come down for breakfast. Did you finish the lounge?"

Maggie drew herself up with a dignity that went oddly with her sagging, dumpy figure.

"Aye, Madam, that I have," she said with smug satisfaction, and, with a friendly smile for Beth, stalked into Mrs. Trevelgen's room.

"If I had my way, that woman would go. She can be most insolent at times," grumbled Sophia as they went downstairs. "And I thought all nurses wore uniforms," she added with a bright vindictive glance at Beth's blue suit that she hadn't had time to change.

That puts me nicely in my place, thought Beth ruefully.

Sophia seated herself at the head of the table with an air of gracious importance.

Beyond a raised eyebrow Ruan went on eating his porridge.

"Good to see you again, Beth," said Gawen, after having enquired after his mother. "Now I can tell you all about our spook. I was interrupted the last time." His mobile mouth went down at the corners as he glanced at his brother. "Did you know the house was haunted?" spooning his grapefruit with gusto.

"Only that you did mention it yesterday before I left."

Gawen hunched himself into his open-necked shirt, a habit of his that was rather like a tortoise.

"It haunts at the full of the moon, as do all self respecting ghosts. It's headless and waves its arms in the most satisfactory way."

Beth felt her scalp creep. If she had been less tired she would have made some derisive remark and let it go at that. As it was, all she succeeded in doing was to look apprehensive as Ah Wing's ghost stories came to mind, and one cannot have lived in the East for long and not have some of its mysticism rub off on to you.

A shiver ran through her and became conscious of Gawen's evident gratification.

"You're pulling my leg," she accused him.

"He is, too, Miss Dexter," Sophia said sharply.

Her husband sat back, hands in pockets, jingling his car keys and loose change, amused blue eyes darting from one face to another.

"Ruan, you have nothing to say?"

"If that sort of thing amuses you, carry on. It doesn't worry me," refusing to be drawn.

Sophia had clenched her hands. "And stop that jingling, Gawen," she said irritably. "It's most annoying."

"I think all old houses should be haunted," Beth said quickly, sorry for Gawen.

Sophia poured the coffee in a disapproving silence.

"The room next to *Maman*'s has been prepared for you, Beth. I'm sure you could do with some sleep." This, unexpectedly, from Ruan.

Beth thanked him and thought what an understatement this was. She was practically asleep on her feet.

"But who will lok after Aunt May?"

"Sophia and Maggie will take on the day nursing," he said calmly, but with a sharp glance at his sister-in-law.

Sophia bridled at this, her dark eyes snapping.

"I'm no good at nursing. You should know that by now and I thought that was the reason you brought Miss Dexter back?"

"The girl's got to have some sleep."

Beth did not delude herself into thinking that this partisan attitude was inspired by anything but the most ulterior of motives on Ruan's part. He was not a man to make gestures to sentiment. It only meant he wanted her kept fit or else he would be obliged to call in a strange nurse.

"Well, I can't be expected to wait

upon you," Sophia said sullenly. "You'll have to make your bed and do your own washing."

"Really, Sophia!" said Ruan angrily. "How can you — "

"It will be me who will be waiting upon Miss Beth and the Mistress," chided Maggie coming into the room.

"You're meant to be upstairs," said Sophia.

"Maggie, you timed that cue perfectly," said Gawen with amusement, but the old woman ignored him.

"The Mistress is awake and wanting her tea."

Beth was glad to be able to escape upstairs and after a careful look at her godmother, who seemed a little brighter, she walked to her room. She slept solidly for eight hours.

★ ★ ★

Two days went by with only a slight improvement in Mrs. Trevelgen's condition, but the old doctor seemed satisfied. Beth nursed her devotedly and spent all her waking hours by her godmother's bedside. Sophia was not a good nurse and more often than not when Beth came back on duty, she found her patient fretful and her temperature up.

One afternoon Ruan came home early and offered to sit with his mother.

"Off you go, Beth," he said. "It's such a lovely day and a walk on the beach will do you good."

He was quite unaware of his sister-in-law's coldly speculative glance as if she had been surprised that he had put himself out at all.

Beth found her on the terrace when she went out a little later.

"It's a lovely old house, isn't it?" Sophia said, her back against the terrace wall.

The sun had silvered the old stone work to a soft, kind grey, the windows bright as jewels.

Sophia's hands were working nervously. She looked ill, thought Beth, with sudden compassion, and even Maggie had remarked that Mistress Sophia was as restless as a spring toad and had suggested she see a doctor, but had had her head snapped off for her pains.

"Yes, it is beautiful this afternoon," Beth said with some reservations.

"It's too big and cold for you, perhaps?"

"Well, after our small, compact bungalow, this is a bit over-powering."

"This will be Denzel's one day; it must be," Sophia went on tensely a fanatical light springing to life in her dark eyes that had come to rest on the shining red-brown hair of the girl next to her.

Beth stared back a little uncertainly.

"But what about Ruan? He'll marry one day."

"No, he won't," a grim certainty in that single sentence. She laughed, a high brittle sound. "Laylia, his fiancée, was very tragically killed, you know."

"Yes, Aunt May told me, but a

person can love again," Beth reminded her.

Sophia shrugged, turning around to face the sea so far below, the cliff edge a hundred different colours.

"Not when one has been jilted as well, not a man of Ruan's stamp anyway. I was the one to tell him about his precious fiancée. The night before the wedding it was too. The two of them running away. Cam and Laylia, running away from a marriage Laylia did not want." Her voice was smug.

A crawling, sickening chill of horror shuddered through Beth. Sophia had managed to infuse an element of sordidness into the meagre details and a maliciousness that smacked of hurt pride, but need she have told him so brutally that his fiancée had been running off with someone else? Surely when she heard of the accident, she could have spared Ruan that and left him with his illusions.

Beth found herself wondering what

this woman had been like nine or ten years ago, before her marriage to Gawen. Had she tried for Ruan's favours first?

Ruan, the Master of Truran, cheating his brother of the inheritance by an hour. His marriage would have meant the end of the road for Sophia and she must have been relieved when Laylia had been so opportunely killed. Death should not really make us bitter, thought Beth, should not pollute our memories, but the thing Laylia had done to Ruan, must have been more than enough to make him eschew the fairer sex.

Ruan's chosen path of loneliness suited Sophia's plans admirably, in fact, it was the only way in which her son could reach the heirship.

Beth tried to fling off the feeling of distaste that had laid hold of her. Sophia, seeing the shiver said abruptly:

"Why don't you go down to the cove? It will be lovely and sheltered there. You haven't been out for days."

"I really should go back to Aunt May. I only came out for a breath of fresh air."

"I'd make use of Ruan's kind offer." The elder woman had drawn closer, peering short-sightedly at Beth, a smile twisting her pale lips, dark eyes dilated.

Beth backed away hurriedly.

"Yes, I think I will." There was something evil about Sophia this afternoon and Beth was glad to be able to run down the narrow twisting stone steps, eager now to be on the beach but at the next bend, she checked her pace. Something had brushed against her bare leg, holding her back.

Beth looked down, but there was nothing there and took another step down. What she did next was instinctive. She flung herself against the cliff face gripping the rock, for the step on which she now stood was rocking dangerously. Beth sat down with legs that trembled and a heart that thudded furiously in her throat. The stone tread was jutting out at least six inches. If she had stepped on it a little nearer the edge, she would have hurtled to the bottom.

Beth pushed the stone back and went soberly down the remaining steps. At the bottom she looked up and saw a flick of green on the terrace above and then the figure disappeared from sight. Sophia had gone into the house.

Beth enjoyed her hour on the beach. This was a delightful cove, resting at the foot of high cliffs that dominated this part of the coast. It gave an impression of utter peace and tranquillity after the turmoil that she had experienced during the last few days. If it had been warmer, she could well have imagined herself back on one of the Singapore beaches, the sand was so white.

Beth reluctantly made her way back up the rocky steps and gingerly missed the loose stone. She must remember to tell Ruan about it. It might work loose again and was positively dangerous as it was at present. A startling thought came to mind. Had the piece of slate covering the step been pulled out deliberately?

Ruan rose to his feet as she came back into the room.

"Thank you, Ruan. It was glorious on the beach," and went on to tell him about the loose stone.

"You had better see to it now, son," said Aunt May, but her glance was for the bright face of the girl with the tranquil grey eyes and reddish gold hair.

"I'll go and see to it now," he promised.

That evening Mrs. Trevelgen took a turn for the worse. She lay very still in the big bed, her face more finely etched than it had been a few days ago, the nose and mouth more prominent.

Maggie slipped in as quiet as a shadow.

"How's the Mistress?" she asked breathlessly, with an anxious glance at the bed, before taking the tray with a steaming cup of coffee and a plate of sandwiches into Beth's room. "I heard the Master ring for the doctor."

She shook her head, her eyes going mesmerically to the interleading door, her whisper full of foreboding. "This is the end. The Hound was seen this evening. My cousin's girl came up with the news not half an hour ago. No fishing boats will venture out tonight."

Beth looked mystified, but before she could ask Maggie what this was all about, Ruan came in.

"The doctor will soon be here. He's on his way." He looked tired and despondent.

"Oh, Master Ruan!" said the old woman, twisting her rheumaticky hands into a knot, tears dimming the bright eyes. "The Mistress is going to die; I know it."

"Rubbish!" said Beth, her voice crisp. "Aunt May is not nearly so ill as she has been. Maggie, what's got into you?"

"It's the Hound, Miss," she said tearfully, with another wild look at the bedroom door.

"Maggie, you're just being silly,"

said Ruan kindly, an arm around the bent shoulders. "My mother is not going to die, if we can help it. Now go and make some more coffee. The doctor will want some."

The doctor arrived and Beth forgot all about Maggie's strange jabbering, but a few hours later, she was to remember them. It was getting on towards midnight and Beth was beginning to get really alarmed again at her godmother's difficult breathing and was just about to go and ring for the doctor, when she heard the click of paws on the bare linoleum in the passage. The dogs weren't allowed upstairs but Rory, the Corgi, had on several occasions sneaked up. She would take him back to the kitchen, but no sleek, brown body came through the door and yet the clicking continued, right across the bedroom floor and suddenly stopped at the mat in front of the fireplace.

Beth shook her head, trying to clear her brain. She must be more tired than she thought, or had she dropped off to sleep for a moment and dreamt those clicking paws, but she was still on her feet. She had just decided that overtiredness can play some queer tricks with one's imagination, when a movement from the bed made her turn sharply to her godmother and Beth was even more puzzled and amazed when Mrs. Trevelgen said in a much stronger voice:

"Dear Shag. Dear Hound of Truran. You've come to see me."

Beth blinked stupidly, mouth hanging open, her eyes going from her godmother to that mat in front of the fireplace. So she had not dreamt those clicking paws. Aunt May had heard them too.

There was a smile on the bloodless lips. "You are not to worry about me, you know. I'm going to get well, but it is nice to have you in your usual place."

Beth's glance went mesmerically back to the mat. Was there just a hint of an indentation in its soft pile, or was this only her imagination. Beth went over to the bed.

The tired, hazed eyes were closed. Mrs. Trevelgen had dropped into the first really peaceful sleep since her accident.

Beth sat back in her chair. The minutes dragged by, her eyes heavy with denied sleep, the quiet room and shaded light having a horrible drowsy effect on her. She must not sleep, for her godmother might wake again.

Beth got up and went to the window, leaning on the sill, drinking in the cool night air. Only the crash of waves against the rocks below broke the stillness and even that was muted for it was low tide. Suddenly a light blinked out there in the darkness. It blinked once, twice, three times and then Beth saw it no more.

On just such a night like this, smugglers, many years ago, had shown their small furtive lights and been answered from the shore. She turned from the window with a smile at her flight of fancy, but her godmother was sleeping peacefully.

Towards morning, Ruan came in, his black hair tousled, his hands deep in his dressing gown pockets.

"How is she?" he asked in a low tone.

"Much better, but we can't talk in here. Come into the other room."

"Her colour is much better, isn't it?"

Beth nodded as she poured milk into a saucepan and placed it on the gas ring.

"I'll watch that," he said, "but what's the matter, Beth? There is a whole host of emotions on your face this morning," his glance keen from under the thick, black brows.

She laughed a little uncertainly.

"You'll think I'm quite crazy, but Aunt May has definitely benefited from her midnight visitor. She — she just dropped off to sleep like a baby."

Ruan turned from the gas ring.

"What visitor?" he asked sharply.

Beth went on mixing the cocoa, the

reddish brown hair falling over her cheeks.

"Your ghost, I presume."

"What? Shag?" he asked in amazement.

"Oh, so it does exist? I did wonder if I'd dreamt it. Ruan, the milk!"

He snatched the saucepan from the flame.

"Oh yes, Shag walks all right, but hasn't done so for some time."

Beth made the cocoa and they sat drinking it.

"Strange that he should appear tonight." His whole tense body suggested the presence of the dog held far more to it than a mere haunting.

"Tell me the story," she invited, her tiredness forgotten. There was a stillness about the room that made for confidences.

"*Maman* rescued him as a pup from a couple of village louts who were tormenting him. He was a scrap of a thing, thin, with ribs sticking out, dirty, flea-ridden. In fact, he was a sorry sight, but *Maman* reared him and

Shag turned out to be quite a dog. A woolly rug of an animal, half Collie, half Alsatian, and I expect a dash of something else for good measure. He was always well loved in the village, especially after he had saved one of the fishermen's children from drowning and now has become something of a legend."

Ruan lit a cigarette, the small flame throwing his features into sharp relief. "After he died, the people hereabout always referred to him as the Hound of Truran, swearing they saw him one evening, high on the crags of Queen's Needle, that tall pillar of rock, standing a little out to sea, and the legend was born." He shrugged. "It could have been merely a cumulus of cloud above the rock and the vivid imagination on the part of one of the villagers, did the rest."

"I certainly did not imagine those clicking paws on the lino, nor did your mother," said Beth, sipping her hot cocoa.

Ruan nodded.

"Oh, I believe you," he said quickly. "He has been heard before. Mother swears Shag came to comfort her the night Father died."

"That would account for Maggie's fear," said Beth and gave a startled gasp, her hand going to her mouth, a gesture that still remained with her from childhood. It had been a dog's body that had held her back on the cliff steps.

Ruan's dark blue eyes were question marks.

"Now what?"

"I'm pretty sure it was Shag who saved me from a nasty fall this afternoon — no," with a look at her watch, "yesterday afternoon. Did you check that loose step?"

"Yes," he said, helping himself to a sandwich that had curled at the corners, "but, Beth, you made a mistake. There was no loose stone."

"But there was," contradicting him sharply. "It was protruding at least

101

six inches and wobbled horribly. Do you think I could make a mistake like that? I was running down those steps pretty quickly, then something held me back, brushing against my legs, and because of that, my next step was more careful and I was able to throw myself against the cliff. If I'd stepped a little nearer the edge of that tread, I'd have had a nasty tumble." She paused seeing Ruan's sceptical face and added lightly. "Perhaps someone wants to get rid of me."

His frown came down over his straight nose, meeting her steady grey eyes impatiently.

"Who'd want to to get rid of you, for Pete's sake! Really, Beth, you haven't been getting enough sleep lately. Once again, there was no loose step. I checked every one."

"I say there was," eyes now sparking smokey grey fire across at him. "You didn't want me here in the first place and you weren't overpleased when I had to come back to Truran House.

You only tolerate my presence because you need a nurse." The words tumbled out without any thought.

Beth drew back, a little afraid of this suddenly grim-faced man across the table from her.

"Your reasoning powers are out of step, my girl," he said through half closed teeth. "It must be the late hour. I need you here, or else I would not have pulled you off that train."

Beth lowered her eyes.

"I'm sorry," she said contritely, "that was an awful thing to have said, but you did say you didn't want me here," her voice accusing.

"Yes, I did, but it was nothing personal." His smile was bitter.

"You mean you wouldn't welcome any woman to Truran House? It wasn't just me?" and when he nodded his head, went on: "Well, thanks for those small crumbs of comfort."

An uneasy pause filled the room.

"I'm sorry you were so badly hurt, Ruan," she said gently.

He shrugged.

"Who told you the sorry tale anyway? Sophia I bet," running a hand through his hair, that was as black as an apple pip.

"Does it matter? Isn't it better to have found out before you were married than afterwards? And, anyway, the world is full of very nice girls, Mr. Trevelgen," she reminded him pertly.

"Yes," he conceded, "but even nice girls are prone to look out for Number One. There's not many tricks a woman won't try, to secure a nice comfortable living," he added cynically.

Beth should have been angry, but she had become used to poisonous barbs during her training and Ruan's insolent words glanced off her harmlessly.

"If that's the attitude you have adopted, perhaps it is just as well you have stayed single," she said calmly, "and if it will make you any more comfortable, I do have a boyfriend, so I'm no threat to your lonely way of life. Kim and I hope to announce our engagement as soon as he has passed his finals."

Beth patted the broad shoulder nearest to her in her most professional manner as if soothing a small, restless boy.

Before she could elude him, he had scooped up her bare left hand with hard fingers.

"He's taking a chance, isn't he?" one eyebrow climbing high in derision. He let her hand drop and lounged comfortably back in his chair, his long legs outstretched as if it were early evening and not four o'clock in the morning. "Fancy him letting you come half across the world without a chunky diamond upon your finger to shout to all and sundry that you belong to him."

Beth turned away from those jibes, away from those dark eyes gleaming so derisively in the shadows cast by the standing lamp in the far corner of the room, her heart twisting. Ah Wing had said something similar before she had left Singapore.

"You don't understand," she said with quiet dignity. "Kim trusts me," and was unprepared for the urgent hands that took her by the shoulders.

"So I don't understand what trust means? Wait until you have had it snatched from you and trampled in the dust like mine was," he said savagely.

For a moment Beth saw herself reflected in his eyes, saw also in those dark blue depths, a terrible agonising bitterness that matched the bitterness of his mouth. Felt a strange and unexpected urge to gather this man to her and try and blot out that dreadful hurt she still sensed in him after all these years.

Ruan dropped his hands from her shoulders.

"I'm sorry," he muttered and Beth watched him disappear through the doorway.

4

IT was a dreary morning with wisps of mist trailing ghost fingers across the high dining-room windows, the half oak panelled walls and heavy maroon curtains adding to the dreariness.

Maggie brought in the breakfast and Beth was again reminded of the light she had seen in the night.

"Did the boats go out after all?" was her query.

The old eyes were keen.

"No, why do you ask, Miss Beth? The fisherfolk do not go out if the Hound has been seen and as you know, he did appear last evening. One of the villagers saw him."

Beth picked up a spoon, trying desperately not to yawn.

"Someone must have been fishing for I saw the light close to Queen's Needle."

"What an eventful night you must have had," cut in Ruan, then turning to the others said, "By the way, the Hound visited *Maman* last night, so Beth tells me."

There was no mistaking Sophia's start of surprise, or Maggie's frightened gasp.

"So, dear old Shag has stalked again," said Gawen, toying with his food.

Sophia's shrug was impatient.

"I think you imagined it, Miss Dexter," she said sourly.

"But, my dear, others have heard him — it," retorted her husband.

"Well, I haven't. I'm not that fanciful. Who ever heard of a dog haunting?"

"Aye, we can say we're unique in that," put in Maggie, with intense satisfaction in every sagging line of her plump figure. It would be her turn to tell the villagers about the Hound and wouldn't she relish that?

Sophia gave a brittle laugh and Beth

108

thought again how tense she was, the fawn twin set deadening the pale face and only the dark eyes had any life to them.

"And what an ugly, underbred dog he was too and not at all affectionate," said Sophia, her mouth twisting.

"Aren't you forgetting how he used to guard Denzel's pram for hours?" asked Gawen.

His wife's rather severe expression softened momentarily.

"Yes, but do you remember how he hated Laylia, Ruan? He'd bare his teeth and growl every time she came near him, or you. I must say though, he showed some sense there," pausing reflectively. "Just as well you didn't marry her, Ruan. Think how uncomfortable it would have been. Not a disapproving mother, but a disapproving dog."

Beth saw Ruan's mouth tighten.

"If I remember rightly, after all these years, old Shag didn't like you either, Sophia," put in Gawen with a chuckle.

His wife went a dull red and Beth though again how ill this woman looked, jumping at every little sound and with an irritating habit of peeling her nails when her hands weren't otherwise occupied.

Gawen yawned.

"Please bring me a glass of water, Maggie, before you go. There's a dear."

He was quite unlike his usual buoyant self this morning, looking as if he could have done with more sleep and kept licking his lips. To Beth he appeared dehydrated and wasn't surprised when he turned to his wife and said accusingly:

"You doctored that coffee last night, Sophia."

"Yes, dear, I did. You complained of a headache so I popped one of the doctor's powders into your coffee. I know how you hate taking them," and gave a little laugh, but her glance was wary. "You're a proper child when it comes to taking medicines."

"Did I have a headache last night?" His manner was vague and he yawned again. "Oh yes, I remember. It was rather a hectic day yesterday, but I don't think I had a headache, only felt a little tired," running a hand through his thick, springy hair as if to clear his head. "Chuck those powders out, Sophia," his tone edged with irascibility. "They make me feel foul."

Beth escaped at the end of the meal and went out on to the terrace and down the steps that led to the small cove. There was something she had to find out. She bent over the step that had been loose and looked at it closely. Ruan was right. It was as firm as its fellows, but her sharp eyes soon picked out the tiny stone wedged in tightly between the rock face and the step.

I know I did not dream it, thought Beth with conviction and a slow shiver of fear inched down her neck. Who had deliberately loosened that stone?

Mrs. Trevelgen's recovery was slow and the doctor still visited her most days, but the night nursing had been dispensed with.

One sunny afternoon Mrs. Trevelgen said firmly:

"Now off you go, dear child, and get some fresh air. You are cooped up here far too much. Maggie will be coming to sit with me, but why I cannot be left to my own devices now and again, is quite beyond me," and her silvery brown eyes sparkled with something of their old brightness.

Beth smiled back, grateful that this dear person had been given back to her.

A few minutes later, Beth ran down the stairs and out of the house. A brisk walk along the headland was just what she needed. She set off, her face turned to the bracing freshness of the wind.

The ocean looked strangely empty this afternoon, the tide far out. In the distance a ship was steaming up the channel. From the Far East, perhaps? Her thoughts winged to Kim. There hadn't been a letter from him, only cables saying how busy he was.

Beth left the path and scrambled up to the highest point of the headland where, in the deep rock-strewn ravine below, the surf foamed and fretted. The high, wild cries of the gulls somehow suited her mood. Turning around she saw Sophia coming along the headland, but Beth was startled when a figure of a man sprang out from behind a stone hedge. He appeared to be very angry and kept gesticulating wildly with his arms, but Sophia must have said something to pacify him for he calmed down and walked away.

That evening Beth was admiring the portraits of the Trevelgens in the high, black-beamed gallery, when Gawen came out of the room to the left.

"Ah ha! Glancing over our ancestors, I see. A redoubtable lot, are they not?" pride in his voice. He went and stood in front of a portrait of a man with a hawk face, hooded eyes and a cynical twist to his hard mouth.

"This is ancestor John," and tilted

his head, pursing his lips. "Now there was a scoundrel, if there ever was one. Lost an eye and an ear in a fight with excisemen, but did that make him give up the profession? Not he! 'Brandy for the parson, baccy for the clerk' as the saying went, was a lucrative trade. It paid for this house. I don't suppose my mother told you that?" His inquisitive blue eyes swept back to her.

"No," smiled Beth.

"She wouldn't. She tries to kid herself that the House of Truran has always been highly respectable. You'll find that *Maman*'s like that. Anything that offends her sense of pride, either in the present or the past, must be wiped away as if it had never been. Ha!" he gave a crack of laughter. "This house was built as a bastion against raiders and then used by smugglers. Nobody can hide that fact."

"I'm sure your father wasn't a smuggler," she said and moved across the room to stand before a portrait of a man, whose likeness to Ruan was startling. The same well-defined, straight brows that lent added strength to the already craggy face, the firm lips and stubborn chin. There was a remarkable likeness to all these Masters of Truran.

Gawen's smile was regretful.

"No, worse luck. We might have been a lot more wealthy if father had gone in for the trade." He turned. "Ah, here comes the present Master now," not a vesture of jealousy in the gaily spoken words as his brother crossed the gallery towards them. Here was a man completely overshadowed and yet it didn't appear to bother him in the least.

"What a pity there is no more smuggling these days," Beth said regretfully. Gawen had gone and Ruan had taken his place.

"I don't think you'd have liked those days," he said repressively. "The reivers of old took what they fancied, be it in women or cargo." The fan lines spread from the corners of his eyes and mouth, the light from a wall bracket deepening each contour, as he mocked her, "but I'd want no unwilling woman."

Sophia had come up the stairs.

"Then you wouldn't be upholding our motto," she jeered. "Take and hold. You did neither, did you, Ruan, as far as Laylia was concerned?" The cruel shaft sped between the thin lips, her eyes cold and malicious.

Sharp, unexpected anger shook Beth and she was surprised that Ruan did not seem at all perturbed, his manner merely indifferent.

"You never wanted me to marry Laylia, did you, Sophia? I wonder why? I remember how very upset you were when we announced our engagement, even going as far as to say we'd never be happy. Did you hope, even then, that one day you would be Mistress of Truran?"

Sophia drew herself up stiffly, anger kindling her dark eyes to a purple fire.

"How dare you say that to me!"

Maggie's treble piped up the stairs and Beth said with relief: "It's time we went down to dinner."

Maggie brought in the roast when the family were seated.

"I don't know what this country is coming to," she grumbled. "There's an awful lot of foreigners around here lately. Had one at my back door only this afternoon, but when I asked him what he wanted, he mumbled something and left."

"But then Maggie's idea of a foreigner is someone from another county, not necessarily from another country," put in Gawen to no-one in particular.

"I saw you having an argument with a man on the cliff path this afternoon, Sophia. He looked foreign. I was just about to come to your assistance. Was he pestering you?"

Sophia's face was expressionless.

"It was just some-one who wanted to know the way to St. Murran, and you know these people's exaggerated ways."

Ruan, who was sitting next to Beth, stiffened.

Fenella arrived the following week and Beth would not have recognised this tall, fair girl with the eyes of a stranger and who held herself like a model. When Fenella had left Singapore, she had been a gangling, shy teenager of fifteen, only interested in clothes that consisted of very brief shorts and suntops, freckles liberally sprinkled over a short nose that was usually in some stage of peeling. Three years had certainly changed Fenella, and Beth did not like the hardness in the blue-green eyes or the casual greeting she received from her sister.

It was a different matter entirely when Ruan came in for tea, for Fenella was the impulsive child Beth had known, as she rushed to greet him, with a gay laugh and even gayer words.

"Oh, it's wonderful to be here again, after I had thought I would have to land up in a stuffy London flat and how is the yacht? I shall want to go sailing just as soon as possible."

"You have grown up, Fen. Last time you were here you hadn't inhibitions. Aren't you going to kiss me, even if it's only for old time's sake."

Beth was amazed at the warmth in his voice, but Fenella side-stepped him neatly.

"I'm not a child any longer, Ruan," she reminded him fiercely and then a slow smile stole across her face. "We were taught that young ladies don't throw themselves at men's heads," but, although her words were prim, her eyes and tilted head were provocative, the long hair as fair as spindrift cascading to her shoulders.

Well, thought Beth with amusement. Her little sister had indeed grown up.

It was only after everyone had gone to bed that night that Beth had an opportunity to talk to her sister alone.

"Must you wear a uniform. It gives me the creeps," were Fenella's first words, uttered with distaste.

"Yes," said Beth firmly. "It gives

a patient confidence and the nurse a certain standing in the house. It's lovely to see you again, Fen, after all these years," she added warmly, "and fun to think we'll be sharing a flat soon. I want to get to know you and I do so want to make a home for you, darling."

"Tell me about the accident," she said abruptly, fiddling with the top button of her gown as if the high collar was choking her.

Beth tried to tell her sister calmly about that fateful day when both their parents had been drowned in a gale, but her voice quivered several times. Fenella never uttered a word, but her hazel eyes had widened in horror as if she, herself, were partaking in her parents' tragedy. At the end she dropped her head in her hands, harsh, dry sobs tearing her body.

With an upsurge of tenderness, Beth gathered the slim figure to her, but Fenella drew herself away.

"Now I'm all alone."

"But darling, we've got each other. We'll get a flat and then see about a career for you."

"You'll get married soon. There's Kim." The fair hair swung across her cheeks. "I should worry," she added defiantly. "I've always been the odd man out."

"How can you say that, Fen."

"Mother and Father didn't really want me — or you either, Beth," with dramatic outflung arms. "They were only too pleased when the time came to send us off to school."

"Fen, I never felt this way," Beth said with swift distress. "We had the most wonderful holidays. You can't deny that."

Fenella refused to meet the pleading grey eyes, pleating the flame coloured gown with trembling fingers.

Beth watched her with a troubled frown. So her godmother had not exaggerated her sister's deep sensitivity.

"I know you didn't want to go away to school, but Fen, believe me, I know

121

your health would have suffered badly if you had stayed in Singapore," but her sister was unconvinced.

"They never wanted any encumbrances and anyway, I was probably a mistake, born five years after you were."

Beth found her patience becoming a little thin.

"There are other reasons for a gap between children," she said almost tartly.

"Oh Beth!" Fenella's full under lip began to tremble ominously. "Now you're cross with me."

"No, I'm not, darling and I think it is time you went to sleep. You are probably tired after your journey. I know how awful I felt."

"You promise you'll not go off and leave me in London by myself?" said Fenella and Beth caught the shaft of fear and uncertainty again in those greeny depths.

"You'll soon find your feet, poppet. We'll talk about a career for you in the morning," Beth said soothingly.

"But I'm not interested in anything." The reply came out stubbornly and childishly.

"You'll have to do something. Father didn't leave much and, because Mum died too, his pension fell away. I've only got what I earn."

Her sister's dismayed face caught at Beth's heartstrings.

"No — no money at all, then we're poor?" Her lips quivered again. "How awful!" She sat up suddenly, her mood changing and said with a wilful toss of the fair hair. "Well, I want a fabulous holiday first."

Beth sighed as she shut the door and went down the passage to her room. No use in reminding Fenella that her year in Switzerland was probably the last wonderful holiday she would have for a long time.

Mrs. Trevelgen improved steadily and was able to get downstairs, Ruan carrying her as easily as he would have done a child.

"Really you know, *Maman*, you're getting a bit too heavy for me," he teased, putting her in an easy chair that Beth had pushed to the big window overlooking the checker board fields with their stone hedges.

His mother chuckled.

"Go on with you," she said, "and please bring me that footstool, dear. The draughts in this house are shocking."

"You mean your legs are too short to meet the floor," he said, placing those small members on a beautifully embroidered covered footstool. "Now I really must go."

Mrs. Trevelgen sighed.

"He's a dear boy, but how I wish he could meet a nice girl and fall in love again. I want happiness for Ruan, like my own married happiness, but his tragic loss seems to have soured his very soul."

No hint that Laylia had played her son false and Beth remembered Gawens' words. "Anything that offends *Maman*'s sense of pride, is wiped away as if it had never been." It must have been a horrible shock when her daughter-in-law to be had run away with another man on the eve of the wedding.

Both Mrs. Trevelgen and Beth were startled as Fenella stormed into the room.

"Where's Ruan?" she demanded.

"He went out ages ago, my dear," said Mrs. Trevelgen, delicate eyebrows raised at Fenella's sullen face.

"I wanted to be taken into St. Ives," flinging herself down on to the window seat, the sunlight catching the pale gold hair.

"You should have caught him earlier then."

"I wasn't up. What am I going to do all morning?" Her query was a pettish wail.

"There's always the beach," suggested Beth, "and it's a lovely day."

"But there are no people. What's the use of a beach without people?" She got up and wandered aimlessly out of the room again and a little while later Beth saw her walking down the avenue.

"Maggie, are you going to visit your niece this afternoon?" asked Mrs. Trevelgen later that morning.

"No, Mistress. Was it something you wanted in the village?"

"No, but I did promise Mrs. Arlow a pattern just before I was taken ill."

"She'll be disappointed if she doesn't get it, tied to that wheelchair of hers. Knitting and gossiping is all that's left to her, poor soul."

"And not minding her own business," cut in Sophia. "She sits in that window of hers and nothing misses her."

"I'll go for you, Aunt May," offered Beth. "It's the house next to the Post Office, isn't it? I've often noticed that silvery headed old lady. She always waves."

"That's her," Sophia nodded acidly.

"Where's Fen?" asked Ruan at lunch.

"I don't know," Beth was forced to

say. "We saw her disappear down the avenue soon after you did."

"Didn't she say where she was going?" he demanded.

"Fenella could have told me not to prepare lunch for her," said Sophia with prim disapproval and Beth longed to leap to her sister's defence, but what was there to say? Nothing could excuse Fenella's bad manners.

"I've never known Fen so restless," put in Aunt May, who, though not sitting up at the table was taking her meal with the rest of the family, a tray across her chair. "It's a difficult age."

"Well, thank goodness we won't have to put up with these bad manners much longer. Beth will have to deal with them," said Sophia.

Ruan's face darkened.

"That wasn't very kind, Sophia. We owe a lot to Beth."

"On her side, are you? Since when?" she sneered.

Beth's cheeks burned. How she hated meal times, although when Mrs.

Trevelgen was present, the various members of the family minded their tongues. How much simpler and easier life would be without Sophia's little barbs.

Beth found Mrs. Arlow charming and stopped to admire the old lady's beautiful knitting. By the time she did manage to get away it was too late for a walk. Sinking behind a stone hedge, Beth sat and enjoyed the peaceful, pastoral scene.

She thought about the conversation with Mrs. Arlow. It had been about foreigners, her dislike of them also evident, but she had gone a step further than Maggie had done. Bending over that wheelchair, her deeply accented voice low and confidential, she had said:

"There's talk here-abouts that these people are not coming into this country legally."

Beth was startled out of her reverie by angry voices. Cautiously raising herself, she peered over the hedge. It was

Sophia and the same man who had accosted her on the cliff path. Beth recognised his bottle-green jersey and black beret.

"I want my money back. Things aren't as I thought." The wind carried the threatening words spoken in French.

Beth did not catch Sophia's reply, but she too appeared angry, and then the next words became even clearer as the man shouted at Sophia's receding back.

"You'll be sorry for this, Madame," his fist angrily raised.

Beth walked slowly back to Truran House, her thoughts in a turmoil, wishing fervently she hadn't eavesdropped.

Sophia's injured and disapproving air was still in evidence that evening when Beth came downstairs.

"I hope Fenella won't be late for dinner, if she comes in at all," she said thin-lipped.

Beth let out a relieved breath when her sister came tripping down the stairs just as Maggie poked her crumpled body around the door and announced dinner.

Gone was the discontent of this morning and in its place a defiant radiance.

They all looked up at her. The blue-green eyes appealed for forgiveness.

"And where have you been all day, may I ask?" demanded Ruan.

"Don't be such an old bear," Fenella said coaxingly, running down the remaining steps to put an arm through his, cuddling close like a warm, friendly kitten, her face buried in his shoulder.

The family sat down to dinner in silence.

Fenella picked up her knife and fork, her long fair hair missing her plate by inches.

"Why am I having something different?"

"That's the lunch you should have had if you'd been here," said Sophia thinly.

Fenella banged down her knife and

fork. A warning frown from Ruan made her pick them up again, but she ate very little and looked about to burst into tears.

"I think you could have told someone you would be out for lunch," said Ruan, mildly.

"I'm not a child any more, Ruan. I'm grown-up now. Why should I have to tell anyone where I'm going and I suppose you mean Beth?" Her voice was truculent, her rebellion like wisps of mist pouring from a sullen sky as she shot an angry glance at her sister and then at Gawen, who, as usual, was enjoying the tense situation, devilment in his lazy smile.

"I absolutely refuse to be a puppet on any string of your making, Beth. Do you hear?" Fenella's voice rose in a shrill tone as she continued, "I'll go my own way, or no way at all."

"Dear, that's telling them," said Maggie, who had come in to hear the last sentence. Fenella rasped back her chair then dashing away her tears she strode towards the door.

Beth winced as Fenella slammed the door behind her.

Ruan brought up a tray of coffee after dinner that night. Beth had been unable to face Sophia's disapproving stare or Gawen's inquisitive amused glances. Of Fenella there was no sign.

Beth had regained some of her composure by the time Ruan came upstairs and she was grateful to him for not bringing up the subject of her sister.

A smile of pleasure lit her godmother's face when he opened the door.

"You're a dear boy, Ruan," she said, sipping the fragrant beverage, "but do stop prowling. You make my neck ache just watching you."

As Ruan sat down she went on a little wistfully.

"But you know, dear, much as I love your little attentions, I do wish you would settle down with a nice girl."

"Spare me, *Maman*. I'm comfortable

as I am," lazily stretching out his long legs.

"Yes, too comfortable," and Beth caught the note of tartness. "It's a pity you can't bachelor it for a while. It might change that attitude of yours towards the opposite sex. Men like their comforts, I've found."

"Whom do you suggest? Beth here?" his glance resting on her with mocking amusement.

"Thanking you kindly, Sir, but I'm otherwise engaged," replied Beth lightly.

"Ah yes, I remember. The boyfriend in Singapore."

Mrs. Trevelgen sighed, regret in the silvery-brown eyes as they rested on her goddaughter and son, but she said briskly:

"Beth has had a letter from Kim Crudden to say he'll soon be here, and we've been able to get a room for him in the village."

"And you didn't even tell us this interesting bit of news at dinner."

"There was no opportunity — "

Ruan nodded slightly. "Other things to discuss, I know," selecting a cigarette and carefully tapping it on his thumb nail.

"Bit of an upset this evening?" his mother asked astutely. "Sophia? I wondered why Beth was so quiet."

"I'm afraid it was Fenella," Beth said apologetically. "She walked in just before dinner, as large as life and as equally unrepentant."

Ruan had risen.

"You'd better marry that young woman off as soon as possible, Beth, otherwise you'll have a packet of trouble. Goodnight, *Maman*, sleep well." He bent to kiss the soft cheek held out to him. "Beth, don't take it too much to heart what Fen said tonight. She was merely being 'anti establishment' and her rebellion and anger wasn't necessarily directed to you personally."

Excusing herself to her godmother, Beth followed him through the door, closing it carefully behind her.

"Could I speak to you for a minute?"

"Sure, come along on to the balcony." He held open the outer door and they stepped into the fragrant night air.

How beautiful it was thought Beth, the stars trying to outshine one another across the dome of the sky and the dim outline of headland and jagged cliffs, mysterious and shadowed. She turned almost reluctantly to the man beside her.

"Ruan, it is time I left Truran House," urgency in the soft voice. "Your mother is so much better and doesn't really need me any more and — and — "

" — and Fenella is getting out of hand," he finished up for her.

"I don't know what got into Fen tonight. I wouldn't have blamed Sophia one bit if she had exploded this evening."

"Stop worrying about it."

Beth was a little indignant at his complete indifference.

"How can I?"

"The girl's probably dreamed of freedom for a long time. Now when she's got it she finds herself surrounded by a lot of grownups who still expect her to conform. We're a lot of squares to her."

"But we all have to conform," she protested quickly.

"Be your age, Beth. With society as permissive as it is today, not all people think like that," he scoffed gently.

"Well, I don't want my sister to travel the road of unconventionality. This worries me stiff and gets us back to the beginning. It's time I left," she said again, a little desperately, not liking the stubborn set of his jaw.

"You'll stay, Beth, until I'm quite sure *Maman* won't have another attack," his hands going to her shoulders, gripping them tightly.

"But, Ruan," she said jerking away from the warmth and strength of his fingers, perturbed at his nearness.

136

"Sophia and Maggie can manage easily now."

"*Maman* does not get on with Sophia. You should know that and she's a rotten nurse."

"So, I'm to be kept here against my will? To *take and hold*, is that what you intend to do with me?" she taunted him.

"Is it really against your will, Beth, or is there relief in those translucent grey eyes of yours that your future has been shelved just a little longer. I've somehow got the impression London isn't quite to your taste."

The moon picked out the mockery in the dark blue eyes holding her own so unmercifully and Beth's glance sidled away uneasily.

"You're quite mistaken," she said coldly. "All I want to do is find a job, make a home for Fenella and start her on some career."

"And she is going to kick like blazes," he warned. "Stay for a little while longer, Beth and I'll try and amuse Fen. That should keep her out of Sophia's hair and stop you worrying. Goodnight," and with an abrupt movement he was gone.

If only some one like Ruan would marry her sister. Those broad shoulders of his would cushion her against cold winds, but he would stand no nonsense either and that was what Fen needed badly just now.

As Beth went back to her godmother she wondered why the idea should please her so little.

5

BETH and Fenella were coming up the cliff steps after having had a bathe when Fenella said abruptly:

"By the way, Beth, what about doing something about handing me over half of the inheritance, or must I go through the solicitor in Singapore. I could do with money right now."

The brightness of the morning was suddenly dimmed for Beth as she turned to her sister in dismay.

"But darling there'll be nothing over when the estate has finally been wound up."

"Then we're really poor?" Fenella paused on the next step, her hand going to the cliff face as if her legs had suddenly deserted her. "Beth how awful! It's all right for you, you've got your nursing."

"As soon as you've gone through Business College, you'll also be earning a salary," she said reasonably, but she saw the idea had little appeal. "Of course I'll let you have some pocket money now, darling."

They had reached the terrace.

"Pocket money!" The inoffensive words were taken up shrilly, the greeny blue eyes glittering angrily. "I've had to make do with a miserly sum all these years and now when I've left school, I'm still to be kept short."

"But Fen, the school laid down the amount of money each student could have and, if I remember correctly, it was certainly on the generous side."

Beth's mouth quirked with amusement. "You may call it an allowance if it will make you any happier, Fen."

"Oh! Yugh!" and with an angry flounce Fenella slammed her door shut. The contemptuous, exasperated exclamation was the most expressive Beth had heard for a long time. The door was suddenly opened again.

140

"You can keep your beastly pocket money," her sister said over-brightly. "I'll ask Ruan to take me shopping. What ever else Ruan may be, he's not at all miserly," and the door was slammed again before Beth could expostulate.

The grey eyes were a little troubled as she went to her room.

During the days that followed, Ruan took Fenella out on several occasions. She danced into Mrs. Trevelgen's room one evening demanding to know how she looked.

Tall and sylph-like she stood, wearing a frock in some diaphanous material, caught in full at the neckline by a rhinestone studded collar, cut away shoulders and it was extremely short, the russet and green of the material matching her sparkling hazel eyes perfectly.

"Fen, you look positively ethereal," was Beth's admiring comment.

"You think Ruan will like me? I've always admired him, you know. He's been my pinup for ages and ages. I have a photo of him and the girls were all madly jealous and envious. It's going to be a super evening." She stretched out one slim leg, sheathed in the shearest of nylons. "I hope you don't mind, Beth, but I helped myself to your stockings. Told you I need money badly. Bye," and with a wave of her hand she was gone.

Mrs. Trevelgen was shocked.

"That child needs a good spanking, but," she added wryly, "at least we know where she will be tonight."

Beth coming from the bathroom much later that night, was brought up short by voices from the hall below.

"Oh Ruan, why don't you let me try and mend that heart of yours? Just a little — please." It was almost a wail and Beth could imagine that slim figure close against Ruan, greeny blue eyes appealing, fair hair caressing those bare shoulders. "You've acted the big brother all evening. I could have screamed."

"You think a few kisses would do the

trick, don't you, Fen. Grow up, girl," amusement in the deep voice and then Beth heard Ruan's goodnight and the shutting of a door downstairs.

Fenella came along the passage, a drooping, disconsolate figure, a butterfly whose wings had been bruised, her face stormy and Beth's heart ached for her.

"I suppose you heard all that?"

"Well, you weren't exactly quiet."

Fenella tossed her long flaxen hair over one shoulder angrily.

"I don't know why I waste my time on Ruan Trevelgen. He's heaps older than I am and a proper stick-in-the-mud," with a note of disgust.

But the next evening she was once more angling for his admiration.

"Sing for us Fen," Ruan said, seemingly unconscious of her flattering advances. He was stretched out lazily in his chair, his coal black hair taking on the glint from the standard lamp in the corner. "Something soothing."

It was a cold miserable evening and

even Fenella seemed quite happy to stay in, the big fire casting a warm glow over the oakbeamed room.

She sat down at the piano, but instead of playing something soothing, played one of the latest pop songs and sang it surprisingly well.

Beth, comfortably ensconced on the window seat, the heavy velvet curtains drawn, her legs tucked under her, was startled by the depth and beauty of her sister's voice. How little she knew about Fenella, unease curling within her again.

The tune changed to a dreamy French one, Fenella's eyes, as soft as a summer's sea, resting on Ruan. She was singing for him and for him alone.

"Very nice, dear child," said Mrs. Trevelgen with appreciation, "but come along now and sit here by me. Maggie has just brought in the tea," her blue veined hands busy amongst the fragile china. She had also noted, not without amusement, her young guest's melting glances thrown at her unresponsive

144

eldest son. If the minx thought to ensnare Ruan by such childish methods, Fenella would soon find herself firmly put in place.

Breakfast the next morning was an uneasy meal and Beth wished, not for the first time, that her godmother could be present.

This morning, Gawen was talking about some improvements he wished to make in the business, but Ruan was opposing them quietly, but firmly.

"Why don't you give Gawen a free hand?" Sophia demanded. Her well built figure in its grey skirt and matching twinset had stiffened. "You treat him like a schoolboy. If we stepped up production, I'm sure we'd be able to sell the extra pottery. You know how popular it is."

"But I have no intention of running into debt because of it," her brother-in-law said calmly going on with his bacon and eggs.

Her dark, burning glance darted to Beth.

"And I suppose you're hoping for something in *Maman*'s will? You've wound her nicely around your little finger, haven't you? Wheedling into her affections, but don't think you can get away with it, Beth."

"That's enough, Sophia," Ruan said sharply, his dark blue eyes glinting under the thick black brows.

"But this place needs all the capital it can get," the elder woman went on hotly. "What's the use of an empty inheritance? I wouldn't wish that on my son."

Ruan cast her a repressive stare.

"Now, now," said Gawen soothingly, yet with an expression alight with unholy anticipation. "You mustn't let that ambition of yours get out of hand, my dear," this to his wife. "After all, you are anticipating rather in advance, aren't you?"

"Anticipating Ruan not getting married, or his death?" Fenella asked sweetly.

A shiver ran through Beth, even

though the morning was a bright one. What had made her sister say that?

Ruan, with a movement of distaste, excused himself and strode from the room, his coffee untouched. Beth would have liked to have done the same — and as for Gawen? How had she ever thought him a placid, unassuming man? He was more like a mischievous gnome dancing on the side lines, enjoying and egging on the highly charged emotions of others, but careful never to become involved himself.

That afternoon Sophia brought up an orange envelope.

"Here's a cable for you, Beth. Who's it from?" unable to keep back the avid curiosity that was consuming her.

Beth's smile mirrored her happy expectancy.

"It must be from Kim," and quickly ripped open the envelope.

"Yes, he's arriving on Tuesday."

Sophia was surprised.

"Who's Kim?"

"A very special friend of mine from Singapore."

"I didn't know you had a fiancé," eyeing the bent tawny head as Beth replaced the sheet of paper in its envelope.

Beth smiled with inward amusement. Had Sophia been under the impression that she was wheedling her way into Ruan's heart as well as her godmother's? The idea was ludicrous, yet it was the only possible explanation for the relief that had just poured through this woman.

6

FIVE days later Kim arrived and during the intervening days Fenella became more and more difficult and at times Beth could have slapped her. Ruan took her out most evenings, but during the day she roamed the house like some restless ghost, annoying Sophia intensely with her lazy ways and even the easy going Maggie shook her head and had been heard to mutter something about young people being so difficult these days and that's what came when parents spared the rod.

Ruan drove Beth and Fenella into St. Geraint the morning of Kim's arrival, tactfully dropping Beth at the station and carrying off a grumbling Fenella.

The train was late and Beth paced the platform in a fever of anticipation, glancing at the clock every couple of minutes. The train slowly steamed into the station at last and there was Kim, half out of the window, his face creased in a grin, looking incredibly handsome, with his blond hair shining above a tanned face and then she was in his arms.

"Surely you haven't heard already that you have passed?" Beth said breathlessly, her eyes going over the beloved face, noticing that he was badly in need of a haircut, then realized, with a sense of shock, that she had forgotten this was the length he usually wore his hair.

Kim was holding her tightly by the arms.

"Couldn't stay away any longer, my sweet. I was just longing for a glimpse of that tawny head of yours and those serene grey eyes. They'll cable me when the results come through," and then went on eagerly. "I've already landed myself a job in London. How's that for a fast worker? Happy now?" pulling her

150

back against him.

Beth laughed tremulously.

"Oh Kim! I've missed you so much. I'd almost forgotten your quick changes of mood."

They walked towards the exit, the small, dingy station the most beautiful place in the whole world, to where Ruan and Fenella were waiting for them in the car park.

Beth introduced Kim and they got into the back of the car, Fenella turning around to stare admiringly as Ruan started up the engine.

"Goodness, but you've a mad tan," she said enviously. "I'd forgotten what one really looked like," and dimpled appreciatively when he riposted:

"And you're as fresh and pretty as an English hedge rose."

Yes, reflected Beth with pride. Her sister did give the impression of extreme innocence and fragility and was a little indignant when Ruan said mockingly:

"Perhaps Mr. Crudden meant you were simple, Fen."

Fenella, however, was in too happy a mood to take exception to this. There was plenty to talk about, both Beth and her sister eagerly plying for all the Singapore news.

When they reached Truran House, both Sophia and Gawen came out to greet the new arrival.

"A bit feudal, isn't it?" murmured Kim with an indifferent glance at the huge, square stone house, with it's high windows and thick oak door.

"Breakfast is ready now," said Sophia, leading the way into the hall and Beth was amazed at the pleasantness of her manner, "but perhaps Mr. Crudden would like a wash first?"

Kim had been seated between Beth and Fenella, a different Fenella who sparkled and monopolized the conversation, but Beth did not mind. It was a relief from her sister's usual morose silences.

"And when are you two going to announce your engagement?" asked Sophia, during one of the few lulls in the conversation.

Beth felt the colour rush to her cheeks and quickly recede as Kim said easily, although she knew he was not best pleased at this intrusion into his private affairs, by the small well-known nerve that beat at the side of his mouth.

"I haven't much to offer any girl, Mrs. Trevelgen. Perhaps Beth has told you I've just taken my finals and it will be quite a time before I can support a wife."

Beth caught Gawen's amused glance and a gust of annoyance shook her at his masterly summing up of the situation. It was as if he had probed deep in her heart and saw the hurt and uncertainty there and she hated him.

Beth only half heard Kim ask Ruan about sailing in these parts and Fenella's breathless request to be allowed to go with him.

Beth took Kim up to meet her godmother, who, after a while, tactfully suggested to Beth that she take him to see their magnificent view.

"Why was that chap so amused at breakfast?" Kim asked opening the door out on to the balcony.

Beth laughed uneasily.

"So you noticed. Gawen's awful the way he seems to batten on other people's feelings."

"Like some outerspace gentleman with antennae only receptive to emotion? Had a fellow like that at the hospital. Devilishly uncomfortable it was too."

For the next hour Beth and Kim talked of many things. Kim's exams, mutual friends, but he did not refer again to the subject nearest to Beth's heart. Eventually she could stand it no longer.

"Kim, what about us?" her tone diffident. "You didn't honestly mean what you said at breakfast, did you? Weren't you just annoyed at being asked such a personal question?"

The tawny green eyes went blank under their sandy overlay, an odd trick he had when he did not like the subject under discussion.

"Darling, I really must get settled in this new job first. I honestly haven't a feather to fly with. Let's leave it there for a while, hmm?" he said persuasively, his arm close around her shoulder.

They were standing overlooking the small cove and both looked down when Fenella appeared on the terrace below, her gay, young voice calling up to them laughingly.

"Come on down, you two. Let's go for a swim. It's such a lovely morning." She had already changed into a swimsuit, a brief affair the exact colour of her eyes and that made her look like a mermaid with that long fair hair cascading to her shoulders.

Beth was troubled as they went back into the house to change and tried to throw off the heavy feeling of disappointment that filled her and could not deny, even to herself, that Kim had been very relieved when Fenella had come, so opportunely, on the scene. Kim, the adroit, was still side-stepping vital issues, remembered too the way his eyes had followed that slim figure below and his warm greeting as he waved to her sister.

The days went by, Kim walking up to the house from the village each morning. Fenella would meet him, hanging on his arm as he pulled her up the last hundred yards of the steep incline and they would arrive laughing and panting. Beth did not always see them arrive for her godmother still needed a great deal of attention at that time of day.

One morning Kim was on the doorstep earlier than usual. He roared up the drive in a car he had hired the previous afternoon and when Beth was called downstairs, was like some eager, small boy longing to show off his new toy.

"Come out with me this morning, Bethie. I want to try out the car and, incidently, I heard that Venables is working over at St. Culver's. Do you remember Venables?" and when she nodded her head went on. "Wonder what made him come to this part of the world. Last time I heard of him he was in Australia. Oh well, I'll hear all the news this morning," he added buoyantly, sweeping a plaster of hair from off his forehead. "Get your bag, Beth. Hurry up, there's a good girl," kissing the tip of her nose.

Beth's smile had faded.

"Kim, I can't come out this early. Aunt May spent a rotten night and, after all, I am on a case and being paid for it."

Fenella had come down the stairs as fresh as the new day, her frock psychedelic bright.

"What's the trouble?" her glance going from Beth's perturbed face to Kim's sullen one.

"Beth won't come out with me, that's all." The shoulders were shrugged under the light blue shirt.

The rainclear eyes were filled with indignation.

157

"Kim, it isn't like that at all. What about going to St. Culver's this afternoon when I'm free?"

Kim turned on his heel, his mouth a stubborn line.

"And what am I going to do this morning?" he flung at her over his shoulder as he reached the door. "No, if you won't come, I'll go now — by myself."

Fenella moved forward eagerly, her fingers coaxingly on his bare arm, holding him back.

"Take me," and smiled up at him saucily. "At least I'll be better than no one and I'll be quite satisfied with the occasional remark."

Kim's good humour was instantly restored.

"Now that is what I call a good idea. All right, Beth?" he asked with a grin. "Darling, it would honestly kill me to hang around here for another morning."

"You don't like your will crossed and that's a fact," smiled Beth, but as

158

she watched them roar away down the avenue, felt a sharp prick of pain. Kim could have waited and taken her this afternoon. After all St. Culver wasn't all that far away and then chided herself for being silly. This way Kim was happy and it did get Fenella out of the house and away from Sophia's chiding tongue.

Just before lunch Kim rang up to say they would not be back until that evening.

Beth turned abruptly away from Gawen's raised eyebrows and did not see them sky even further when Ruan said rather unexpectedly:

"Like to come into St. Ives with me this afternoon, Beth?"

"Yes, I would, thank you. I love St. Ives. It is so different from all the other towns around here," a glow of gratitude towards him for being so thoughtful, but Sophia viewed the invitation in quite a different light.

Beth was just about to go upstairs to settle her godmother for her afternoon nap, when Sophia came out of the diningroom, her dark eyes hazed, her thin lips working.

"Aren't you woman enough to fight for the man you love?" she hissed fiercely.

Beth stepped back from this sudden onslaught.

"Fenella has merely gone with Kim because I was unable to do so, and — "

"Well, if you can't see what's going on under your nose — " the elder woman shrugged, "but leave Ruan alone." Her voice had risen again. "Perhaps you aren't the little innocent you would lead us to believe. Perhaps you think, Ruan, Master of Truran, a far better catch than that insipid young doctor of yours. Is that the game you're playing?"

Beth could only stand and stare at the eyes blazing so uncannily.

"You'll never become Mistress of Truran. Never! When my son comes of age, this will be his," with a wave of the hand at the huge stone fireplace and handsome sweep of the staircase that rose up majestically from the hall.

"But Sophia — "

"Don't bleat 'Oh Sophia' at me." There was a curious drawn look about her as if the skin was too tightly stretched across the square jaw and high cheek bones and Beth turned around with relief when Maggie appeared in the doorway, arms akimbo, her round, pouched face flushed.

"I heard what you said to Miss Beth, Miss Sophia. Shame on you and let the Master be. It's a grand thing for him to be taking out a nice girl like our Miss Beth," with a freedom of speech of long association. "And how can you expect Master Ruan not to ever marry?"

"This belongs to Denzel," Sophia said in a strangely quiet way, her gaze going around the oak panelled rooms to rest on the massive, brass hinged door that glowed warmly from the afternoon sun.

"And if he's set his heart on something else? What then?" demanded

161

Maggie. "A lot of young people would not say 'thank you' for being buried alive down here with responsibilities of a large estate and very little money." The rich Cornish accent rolled out. "Or do you really want Truran House for yourself, Miss Sophia? To be absolute mistress here?" She stabbed a crooked rheumaticky finger. "You're afraid that if Ruan marries, his wife will not allow you to stay here and you might be reduced to living in some small suburban house or even a cobwalled cottage. That wouldn't suit you, would it?"

"How dare you! How dare you butt into a private conversation," stuttered Sophia, now mottled with rage.

Maggie turned a kindly eye on Beth, but her words were again directed to the older woman.

"When I came through that door, the poor dear was just gauping like a fish and I'm not surprised, but you can't hush me up, Miss Sophia. I've been here too long."

"Much too long," took up Sophia savagely. "You'll be the first to go when *Maman* dies."

Maggie was unperturbed.

"Oh, aye! I can well believe that and, what's more, I would not want to work for you, Ma'am, but it will not be for a long time yet, praise be and it's thanks to Miss Beth here." With another kindly smile at Beth, she disappeared in the direction of the kitchen.

Sophia turned on Beth her words malicious.

"You've wheedled your way in here properly, haven't you?"

"I'm leaving just as soon as Aunt May is well again," was all Beth found to say.

The hooded lids dropped over the dark eyes and muttering something Beth could not catch, Sophia stormed out of the room.

Beth enjoyed the drive into St. Ives, even though Ruan barely spoke the whole way there, but she was content to watch the countryside go by, the green pasture lands bounded by stone hedges, occasionally throwing an unobtrusive glance at the set profile next to her and wished she could ease that trace of strain on those tight lips.

Beth leaned forward impulsively.

"Be happy, Ruan, just for this afternoon. You needn't be on your guard with me." Her lips tilted michievously. "I've no designs on you, even though Sophia may think differently."

His eyes met hers for a second before turning back to the road.

"No, because of Crudden, I don't have to, do I?" he said and Beth wondered at the unreadable expression she had caught.

They reached the outskirts of St. Ives, nosed up a series of steep bends and parked in a quiet side street.

"Meet you at the Silver Bowl at four o'clock," Ruan said, locking the car door. "I must get a hair cut."

The dark hair was already short by today's standards.

164

St. Ives fascinated Beth. The houses seemed to vie with one another to be different, the gaily painted doors approached by either going up a flight of steps or descending below the level of the road. She spent a happy hour shopping, Kim and Fenella forgotten in her joy at the tucked away shops she came upon quite by chance.

Ruan proved a charming companion. He had sloughed off his old tacturnity as they strolled along the front, past the boats lying at anchor, their bright paint patches of colour against a now darkening sky, the gulls riding in on the waves.

"Would you like some tea, or would you rather go home?"

"I'd like some now, please." Her mouth curved up in a wide, friendly smile.

Ruan watched her pour out the tea from a small tubby brown teapot.

"You're happy this afternoon, aren't you, Beth?"

"Yes, shouldn't I be?"

"It must have been a disappointment that you couldn't go with Kim this morning?"

"Was that why you asked me to go with you to St. Ives?"

"Partly. Beth, don't get hurt." His voice was suddenly harsh.

The grey eyes smiled at him again.

"Where there is love, there's trust, Ruan," she reminded him with quiet dignity. "I'll never forget the love my parents had for each other. At parties or functions they would look for each other. A swift smile, a tender look — that is what I believe love is like."

"And they probably rendered you a big disservice thereby," he retorted cynically.

"Oh, what do you mean by that?" she said with swift distress.

"They were lucky. You're too trusting, Beth. Not everyone is like that," he warned.

Beth's glance met his steadily.

"I know you were badly let down, Ruan and have no illusions left, but haven't you ever felt the need of love in your life? Wouldn't you like a son to carry on the line?"

"I have Denzel." There was only indifference in the quietly spoken words, not even the slightest suggestion of regret or longing — nothing. The hard shell with which he had cocooned his hurt was inviolate and he had no intention of letting it crack, not even for a passing moment.

"Don't you think it would be kinder to Sophia? At the present she's breaking herself to pieces. Any woman who comes within your orbit is suspect, a potential threat to her son's inheritance, even me and it's not right." Her smile was rueful. "If you were to marry, Sophia would probably be a different person."

"I wonder! I suppose I shouldn't have told her that I had made Denzel my heir. In fact, I've regretted it ever since," he admitted, then with a shrug added. "It's too late now."

A loud clap of thunder made

Ruan gulp down the remainder of his second cup of tea and when they came out of the cafe, Beth was surprised how quickly the whole scene had changed. The dull surface of the sea was a running pewter, the waves mountainous and an unnatural calm lay over the town.

7

"WE'D better get home quickly," said Ruan, taking her by the arm and they ran back to the parked car, flashes of lightning ripping the dark swirls of angry cloud to shreds.

He turned on the ignition.

"Love is like that," he said broodingly as the heavens were split open again. "It strikes where it will."

"Stop it, Ruan," said Beth nervously. "Please don't talk like that. I hate storms, anyway," but he went on as if she hadn't spoken, another spear of light unzipping the dark clouds.

"For some there is the magnificence and the lasting joy. Your parents for example. For others — " he shrugged, "it marks in a cruel way."

Beth cowered in her seat as another brilliant flash made the sky, momentarily, as bright as day.

"Cornwall enjoys a remarkably equable and temperate climate, so the guide books tell us," she could not help remarking with an uneasy glance at the churning mass of purple clouds. There was nothing equable or temperate about the electric storm that raged above them. Beth's hand went to her cheek in a childish gesture of fright, her lips quivering and ducked again as a peal of thunder shook the car.

"Mum and Dad were out in a storm like this, in a flimsy yacht. Oh! Oh, I can't bear it, not any more. They're dead," she cried wildly.

Ruan stopped the car and gathered her close into his arms, letting her sob out her grief and fright.

"Did you cry after their death, Beth?" he asked quietly, when her sobs had eased.

She shook her head and drew away from him accepting the handkerchief he held out to her.

"I'm sorry. I told you I hated

storms." She was still shivering with nervous reaction.

Ruan peered out of the window.

"Here comes the rain. The thunder and lightning should get less now."

They watched it sweep down the headland, blotting out everything in its path and then they were in the midst of it.

"Can't drive in this," Ruan said, his eyes on the windscreen that was curtained with swiftly flowing water, the headlights a pale glow, visibility nil.

Beth had no idea how long they sat there, only knowing that she was strangely content. Her own wild storm had blown itself out.

When they finally reached Truran House, it was to find that Kim and Fenella had arrived before them and were enjoying pre-dinner drinks with the rest of the family.

"You're late," was Sophia's comment.

"I'm sorry," said Beth quickly, "but the storm held us up." Though the words were directed to Sophia, her eyes had gone to Kim anxiously. Was he thinking it odd that she had spent the afternoon with Ruan, but all he said was:

"We just missed it, thank goodness," with an expressive wave of the hand.

"Were you hoping he would be just a little jealous?" mocked Ruan, in an undertone as they went through into dinner.

* * *

The following afternoon Kim was at his most charming as he and Beth explored the countryside, but as the days passed Beth began to sense a restlessness in him that was disquietening. He spent less time at the house and often went out sailing, a sport of which he was particularly fond.

Ruan watched Beth's hurt and bewildered face, a grim tightness to his mouth and then one afternoon he had gone into St. Ives and had come across Fenella and Kim in a small cafe. They were sitting close together and did not even see him although he passed quite close to their table. He strode out again, but that evening he called Fenella into his office.

When she was seated, he said evenly, blue eyes dark under the accentuated brows.

"I'm sure your guilty conscience will tell you what I'm about to say to you, Fenella."

She pretended to look mystified, but lowered her eyes when he said abruptly:

"I saw you and Kim in that cafe, this afternoon."

Fenella's hands clenched tightly in her lap, a silence filling the cabinet-lined room.

"Kim and Beth aren't engaged," she reminded him cooly.

Ruan's face was cold, his long, supple fingers fiddling with a pencil which he suddenly threw on to the table.

173

"I don't suppose it would make a scrap of difference to you if they were. Leave Kim alone."

Fenella tossed the gold-white hair over her shoulder and slowly crossed one slim leg over the other as she considered him, a calculating gleam in her green eyes.

"I thought it would have suited you very nicely," she said insolently. "You're interested, interested in Beth, aren't you? Or have I read my signs incorrectly?"

Only amusement lit the dark blue eyes of the man opposite.

"Showing your claws, Fen, because I wouldn't play your little game? I promised Beth I would amuse you. What more did you expect, my girl?"

"You're a cold fish, Ruan, to ask me that," she said scathingly. "Who wants to be treated like a kid sister?"

"I prefer a woman a little more mature than you are," he said carelessly, "and one who doesn't poach on some-one else's preserves. I find that despicable, especially when it involves your own sister."

Fenella jumped to her feet, eyes blazing down at him, the colour so intense that the whites appeared to take on a greeny-gold reflection. She turned, but paused at the door, arms thrown wide.

"And to think I had a crush on you at one time!" The words were spat out angrily. "What do you know of love?" she demanded fiercely. "You, who have been a stranger to that emotion for so long? I want a man whose heart is in the right place, Ruan. You're petrified stone."

Fenella rushed upstairs, a seething mass of mixed emotions and was just about to open her door when Beth came along the passage, on her way downstairs.

"Aunt May wants to see you."

With a moue of displeasure, Fenella brushed past her and entered the room. Mrs. Trevelgen, seated by the fire, eyed her with marked disapproval, marvelling at the difference between the two girls. Almost as great a difference as there was between her own sons. Same upbringing, same environment, but two vastly different products. Beth, with her quiet, charming personality and deep compassion for suffering humanity; Fenella, a piece of quicksilver, rebellious, moody and selfish.

"Fenella," said Mrs. Trevelgen severely, "I've heard some disturbing reports about you."

"What reports? I — I suppose Ruan told you?" Fenella said childishly, her glance fixed on the snowy white hair, hazel eyes refusing to meet those of the older woman, full under lip trembling.

"No Maggie heard it in the village. You're paying too much attention to that young doctor. I shouldn't have to say this, Fen."

"Oh, please Aunt May, not you too." The words tumbled out in a wail. "I've taken all I can from Ruan — please." She flung herself on the floor and buried her head in the soft lap. "Why shouldn't I go out with Kim? Beth can't always go and I get so bored here," and burst into a flood of angry tears. "Now you're against me too. I can feel it," raising a tear smudged face, her eyes wide with hurt.

"Rubbish!" Mrs. Trevelgen said tartly. "If you're not old enough to take a little scolding — " She stopped and sighed, gathering the girl close against her. "Kim, after all, dear child, is Beth's boyfriend."

That evening Aunt May told Beth firmly it was time she had dinner with her family.

"They're getting shockingly out of hand so please help me dress."

Half an hour later they went downstairs to find the family already gathered in the hall. Ruan was propped against the window sill, a favourite position of his, legs outstretched. Sophia and Gawen were sitting, almost primly side by side on the small couch and Fenella? Beth caught her breath. Her sister had changed into a frock of black chiffon with much embroidery at neck and wrists, her fair hair a mist of loveliness piled on top of her shapely little head. A woman's eyes met hers across the room.

Fenella, the child, had gone for good. What had caused this transition?

When Kim walked in a few minutes later, Fenella greeted him coolly, then turned her attention back to Aunt May and didn't glance in his direction again as he took a chair next to Beth.

"And what are you all doing this evening?" asked Mrs. Trevelgen brightly, her birdlike stare darting from one to another.

Fenella grimaced.

"No plans," said Kim easily. "Beth, any ideas?"

"I think you should make a foursome and go out somewhere," Aunt May suggested and did not fail to see the dismayed look that passed between Fenella and Kim. Her mouth tightened. She had been right to come back into circulation. Had these two made other plans? "Ruan?"

"Suits me," he said, stubbing out his cigarette lazily. "I think Beth deserves a night out, if you can spare her, *Maman*. Sophia or Maggie could help you to bed." The dark blue eyes, so full of amusement, turned to Fenella. There was no doubt in his mind that she had had no intention of spending a quiet evening at home.

"Oh, Aunt May! Why a foursome?" Fenella pouted. "I don't mind going out with Ruan at all and I'm sure Beth and Kim would rather be on their own." Her greeny-gold eyes taunted Ruan as if to say "There, aren't I being good?"

"I think a foursome would be nice," put in Kim quickly. "Don't you, Beth? We could go dancing."

Beth agreed, but a shaft of disappointment went through her that Kim had not taken Fenella's suggestion that they go off by themselves. She saw so little of Kim these days.

They left soon after dinner, all piling into Ruan's car. The night spot he took them to was both informal and charming. The band was playing one of the latest song hits when they arrived and Fenella quickly grabbed Kim's arm and said eagerly:

"Beth, you don't mind, do you? Ruan won't dance to these new numbers and you don't like pop all that much."

Beth smiled her consent and found herself comparing these two men. Kim suddenly seemed immature beside Ruan, then scolded herself. Of course he would be. Ruan was six years Kim's senior and Beth could never imagine Ruan dancing with the abandon that Kim was displaying now as he and Fenella twisted and shook to the mad beat of the music.

"I feel positively old, just watching them," she smiled.

"Dear me, Ma'am, and you with never a grey hair to that tawny head," he jeered. "Come along," he added, standing up. "If you don't mind doing a sedate foxtrot to this, I'll have a go, but don't expect me to prance around like those two are doing."

"Dear me, Sir, and you with never a rheumaticky bone in your body," she mimicked.

He laughed as he drew her into his arms. He should laugh more, thought Beth, for it changed his whole face.

The evening sped on, but after Fenella had shanghied an uncomplaining Kim for the fourth consecutive dance, Ruan could not help saying explosively:

"That sister of yours is a menace the way she absorbs excitement and passes it on in triple waves."

Beth glanced across the floor to her sister. There was certainly a feverishness about her tonight, her eyes sparkling, those changeable eyes, sometimes blue-green, sometimes green-gold, depending on her mood, but despite the powerful current of magnetism, she also had a charming air of fragility, wholly feminine and liable to stir a responding chord in any man. Beth couldn't really blame Kim for that admiration he was lavishing on her sister.

Ruan stubbed out his cigarette with a savage movement, his black hair glinting as it caught the subdued lighting on the wall.

"Did you know Fenella was seeing rather a lot of Crudden?" he asked bluntly.

"Is she?" Beth was noncommittal.

Ruan's hand came down over the unsteady fingers playing with a spoon.

"Why this wilful turning a blind eye to what's going on?" he demanded, "or have you had ample experience of Crudden's liking of the opposite sex?"

Beth's gaze flew to his angry one, taken aback by his perspicuity.

"Ruan, I don't think it has anything to do with you," she said quietly, her grey eyes steady.

"Only that I would stop any creature from hurling itself over a precipice," he replied swiftly.

8

THE band was playing yet another song hit, the drummer's sticks frenziedly beating out a mad rhythm. It seemed to Beth that her smile was permanently pinned to her face and she longed for the evening to end. The pink and silver decor that had been so pleasing to her eye at the beginning of the evening, now only seemed garish.

Ruan, watching the expressive face, was suddenly afraid for this girl with the clear grey eyes as a flood of memories mocked him. Beth was at least being given a warning. One had only to watch Kim and Fenella out there on the dance floor to know that Kim would have no scruples about pushing Beth out of his life, if and when he desired it, whereas he had been given no such warning, but would he have heeded if there had been? Perhaps he too would have been blind as this girl opposite him appeared to be.

How he had loved Laylia, a passionate, blind love of youth and how beautiful she had been, with a wild gypsy beauty that had drawn him to her like a moth to a flame. Dark hair drawn back to reveal small, shell-like ears, pointed chin and dark eyes that always had teased him. Fire had flowed through his veins then, as the sweet tormentor had worked her wiles and then came the news that she had been killed in a car accident over at Wanporth.

It had been Sophia, he remembered now, who had come to him in his dark misery of loneliness and despair, to tell him, with stark hatred and malicious satisfaction that his precious Laylia had been in the act of running away with another man on the eve of their wedding. He could have struck her then.

Had Sophia hated him because of

Laylia? Sophia who had lived on the other side of the village, had, in those days, been a handsome girl. How scathing she had been when he had started taking Laylia out and wondered if she had been in love with him herself. Perhaps, even then, she had wanted to become Mistress of Truran, but he had had eyes only for Laylia, that sprite of a girl who had danced into his life one summer evening.

It had been after they had announced their engagement that Sophia had accepted Gawen who had loved her for a long time. Poor Gawen! Ruan thought with a twist of pity for his brother and with a start came back to the present to find Beth gazing at him with concern.

"Sorry, Beth," he said ruefully, running a hand over his eyes as if to wipe away the unsavoury memories. "One should never look back."

"But Ruan, it happened such a long time ago," she said gently.

"You're very young, aren't you?"

with nicely calculated sarcasm. "Young and trusting and able to pigeon-hole other people's problems, their reactions, or so you think."

"Is that such a terrible thing — to be young and trusting?" she protested.

Ruan's glance went to the curve of her cheek, the dark lashes shadows on the tanned skin, a curious pain in his eyes.

"I shouldn't have said that," he apologised. "Guard that youth, Beth and that trusting appeal. I'm just jealous, jealous of my own lost youth and the clock that cannot be turned back." His smile was crooked. "The years the locusts have eaten," he added sombrely. "Maggie said that once to me."

Both turned to face him again, grey eyes wide and very dark.

"I cannot let that pass. The remedy is in your hands," she reminded him. "You make it sound as if there is no further hope of happiness for you and that's a load of rubbish."

186

Ruan lit a cigarette, bending his dark head to meet the flame, mockery reflected again in the blue eyes.

"Don't worry about me. Worry about yourself. Aren't you afraid Fen will take Kim away from you? She's trying her darndest."

A silence spanned between them, and then her uncertainty peeped through for the first time that evening as she watched the two figures on the far side of the room, twisting to the hot beat of the drums that seemed to be beating on the taut nerves of her whole body.

"Kim has always been a person needing a great many human contacts. I've always accepted that; he's just that kind of person," she said slowly.

"Trying to whistle in the dark?" he jeered. "Just because you are loyal and sweet, doesn't mean Crudden will play fair. I reckon he's nothing but a playboy. Have you two made any definite plans?"

Beth stiffened.

"He's not a playboy. He's a most

successful doctor and one who was highly thought of at the hospital where he trained."

Ruan was unimpressed.

"Wrong approach, evidently," drawing hard on his cigarette. "I should have known you would leap to his defence."

Beth glared at him furiously.

"All right! All right! I'm sorry," he grinned, "but from what I've seen of Kim, he's too easy going for you to run happily in his harness, my girl." He paused reflectively. "You'll no doubt hate me even more for this, but do you know what I think? I don't think you really love him at all, or else, why don't you show a little natural jealousy and tell that green eyed, fair haired sister of yours to keep her hands off your property."

Beth's first reaction was to cry out a swift denial but the words would not come. Her passionate protest would merely hide her own deep-seated disquiet that one day Kim would walk away, a disquiet that had often made her wonder what Kim, the gay fun loving young medical student had seen in her, Beth Dexter, a rather shy person with a natural longing for someone to love her, for a settled home, a family.

Beth turned back to Ruan a little helplessly, tracing a pattern on the white tablecloth with the salt cellar. She was being caught in a vortex over which she had no control, while the stage was being set for the next scene.

"You told me once that it was better for the break to come before marriage," Ruan went on gently, his hand comforting the restless fingers. "Look at those two over there. No one else exists as far as they are concerned."

Beth made herself watch her sister and Kim again. Fenella, eager, hungry for life that was just beginning. This urge shone through her eyes as they rested on Kim, provocative, revealing. Beth turned away shocked at those blatant, naked emotions. Did Fenella have no sense of shame?

The next number was a waltz and Kim pulled Beth to her feet, leaving Fenella facing Ruan over the table, a defiant, sullen Fenella, who refused his invitation to dance.

"You need a good spanking, Fen," he said quietly.

"You don't know what it is to be alive," she retorted hotly, "so you can't talk. There's a lump of ice where your heart is."

"So you've said before."

"I'm not afraid to show my feelings," with a defiant toss of her fair hair.

"How would you feel if someone took away the person you loved, Fen? It's always a good idea to put yourself into the other person's shoes and see how you'd like it."

The soft mouth quivered like a child's.

"I think I'd die," she whispered tersely. "I love Kim. He's gay and alive and fun to be with. He understands me

190

like no-one else has ever done."

"Then you'll just have to fall out of love again," he said hardily. "It's merely because he's the most eligible man on the spot, but what of Beth?"

"Oh, Beth!" Fenella shrugged impatiently. "If Kim really loved her, they would have been engaged by now."

Kim's goodnight kiss left Beth strangely unmoved. It had been a hurried, unsatisfying kiss, with Ruan and Fenella in the back-ground and then Kim was gone with a gay wave of the hand and a roar from the exhaust of the sports car he had hired.

Two evenings later Kim left for London to take up an appointment in one of the big hospitals. He had spent the morning sailing and in the afternoon had taken Beth out for a drive, but, already he was walking the wards of St. Joseph's, his mood one of effervescent gaiety and eagerness and Beth knew with a pang that he had been more than bored these last few weeks.

His kiss was long and ardent when he said goodbye. Here was the old Kim back, enthusiastic, gay, but as Beth watched the train recede from sight, couldn't help wondering if it wasn't the backwash of his intense relief to be on the move again. Everything would be all right once he started working, she told herself firmly.

After Kim had gone, Fenella once again roamed the house and Beth was very grateful for the occasions when Ruan took her with him into St. Geraint.

A few days later she came flying out, breathless and excited, on to the terrace where Mrs. Trevelgen was comfortably ensconced in an easy chair, enjoying the spring sunshine and the restful view of fields and tucked away grey cottages.

"Aunt May! Beth! The most wonderful thing! I've had a letter from a friend asking me to stay with her for a week. Here's the letter. Oh, please may I go?"

"How nice for you, dear child. Just when you were bored to distraction," the hazel eyes twinkling mischievously. "Where does this friend live?" asked Mrs. Trevelgen, taking the eagerly held out letter.

"About twenty miles outside London, I think. They've a super house. Sonia often used to speak about it."

"What do you think, Beth?" asked Aunt May, taking off her glasses and replacing them in their case.

"I think it's a lovely idea," she agreed and watched her sister rush away, saying over her shoulder that she would send a telegram immediately.

★ ★ ★

Fenella had been gone nearly a week, a quiet, uneventful week and then one afternoon Ruan handed Beth a telegram.

She smiled as she opened it.

"I suppose it's from Fen to say when we can expect her back." Her eyes went to the words and then her body crumpled, the sheet of paper fluttering to the floor from nerveless fingers.

Ruan quickly picked it up and read the ominous message.

Married this morning. Flying to America tonight. Forgive us. Love Fen and Kim.

Love, he thought angrily, watching the closed face of the girl beside him, so unnaturally still. The thickly lashed lids veiled the grey eyes and only a convulsive movement of her throat betrayed the strain she was under.

"Beth!" he said gripping her by the arms as she swayed.

"Fen and Kim — there must be some mistake," she pleaded desperately and gazed unseeing at the heavy oak door. Her eyes came back to him, bewildered, seeking a reassurance he was unable to give.

All he could do was shake his head and say grimly: "There has been no mistake."

The tears came then, unable to be denied any longer and Beth turned blindly into Ruan's shoulder.

He led her upstairs and opened the door of his mother's room.

"*Maman*, Beth needs you. Fen and Kim got married this morning."

Although Mrs. Trevelgen was shocked, she didn't appear at all surprised.

"Bring us some tea, dear," was all she said, taking her god-daughter by the arm and leading her to a chair.

What words were there to offer, thought Aunt May sadly. That she was sorry? That would be insincere, for Kim Crudden had not impressed her very favourably. It was better this way, but one did not say that to a person who had just been knocked sideways, so Mrs. Trevelgen remained silent, but Beth could feel her godmother's sympathy pouring over her hurt and was grateful that she offered no trite platitudes.

Obediently Beth drank the tea Ruan handed her.

"I think I'll go to bed," she said dully after a while.

"Try and sleep, dear child," said Mrs. Trevelgen.

Beth kicked off her shoes and sank on to the dressing table stool.

"Oh, Kim!" pressing her fingers to her lips to stifle the rasping noise coming from her throat. "Why didn't you tell me you didn't love me any more. I would have understood." Her whisper sounded strange in her ears.

She looked dully at herself in the old-fashioned mirror. Her eyes, the colour of a tossed sea, the straight nose and brown hair, even with its hint of copper, had nothing very spectacular about them, she decided and the answer to her oft repeated question was suddenly made clear.

Kim had chosen her for just a little while, because he knew she would not be a distracting influence, or be very demanding, in those important months before he wrote his finals, a buffer too against the wiles of other women. He had wanted and needed stability and calmness, both qualities she had been able to give him.

Beth moved restlessly on the stool, sparing herself nothing, willing herself to be even more honest. Beth Dexter, a mother image! That's what she had been and Kim had used her shamelessly. It was a lowering thought but the blame was not all his. She should have had the courage, long ago to break with Kim, knowing how she felt, knowing his reputation, but no, she had been so proud that he had chosen her and the hope had always been there that she would be his last love.

Beth went across to the bed, but did not know how long she lay there, staring blankly at the rose-patterned wall, a dull emptiness where once her heart had been. Someone came into the room and pulled the eiderdown over her. It must be her godmother but Beth made no move and at last she slept.

She awoke hours later to find that

night had filled the room. Switching on the light she undressed. The door opened and her godmother came in.

"Aunt May, you should be in bed."

"Saw the light under your door, dear child. The tables are turned," snowy white head cocked humourously. "The patient now visits the nurse. Would you like something to eat?"

"I've had some water. I had a horrid taste in my mouth when I woke up, but I would love a cup of tea and please don't doctor it this time," Beth grimaced.

"But do you think you'll be able to sleep again?" Her godmother's tone was anxious.

"Does it matter? I've got to face this, sooner or later. Tonight is as good a time as any."

"But, dear child. Night reasoning is so much worse than daytime common sense," Aunt May said quaintly. "I never try to grapple with problems at night. They somehow assume ogre-like proportions. I'll go and get that tea."

She was soon back.

They sat sipping their tea and after a while Beth said abruptly: "What I can't understand, or forgive, is why Kim did not tell me while he was here. This one point sticks like a gramophone needle."

"Some people never like to face up to their obligations. Kim is one of them. As far as he was concerned, it was far easier and not so uncomfortable, just to send a telegram."

9

THE next afternoon Beth was on the beach, but hadn't been there long when Ruan joined her, open-necked shirt showing the strong column of his throat.

"Saw you from the terrace," he said easily. "How are things?" falling into step with her, his foot-prints huge in the damp sand.

"As well as can be expected." Her lips twisted a little at the well known phrase so often used by hospital authorities, but his next words caught her unawares.

"Did you really think he would settle for a domesticated life?" he asked abruptly, not liking the drawn lines of suffering on the young face, or the lifeless quality of the grey eyes.

"He married Fen."

"Yes, and I think they'll deal

extremely well together. They'll roam the world with never a feather of responsibility between them. Kim would never have made you happy, Beth and I do give him credit for seeing it before it was too late."

Beth drew away sharply, pulling her towelling wrap around her slim body.

"What does it matter now?" she said tightly and began to walk away, but he caught her by the shoulders, pinning her against the sun warmed rock.

"Face up to this, Beth. Admit I'm right. Admit that you have often had doubts. You must have had, knowing Crudden," he added roughly.

"What can I say?" It came out like a cry of pain.

"If you think it would be disloyal, forget it. You owe no loyalty to the likes of Kim Crudden, or are you afraid to admit that your judgment was at fault?"

Ruan had come very close to the core of the matter, for her grief was not all for Kim's defection — hadn't she always feared that one day he would walk out of her life — but for the betrayal of her innerself. It was as if her heart had turned traitor and had seduced her innocent and trusting nature by foisting on her, in the guise of love, mere infatuation. How would she ever be able to trust that organ again not to lead her astray?

"What are you trying to do to me?" she whispered, through lips that had gone stiff, grey eyes wide with hurt. He had flicked so cruelly at the wound and she suddenly longed for the dullness of shock that had anaethetised her yesterday.

"They say confession is good for the soul."

Beth wondered, with sharpened perception, whether he mocked himself or her.

"I know what you are feeling," he went on. "Humiliated to the very centre of your being, but, Beth, don't let it deteriorate into bitterness. It eats into your very soul. All happy memories become tainted and suspect. I know, to my detriment, what a long lonely road that can be."

Beth could feel the urgency in his fingers as they gripped her shoulders and looked into eyes that were deep, fern-fringed pools, brooding and inscrutable.

He was shaking her now.

"I'm trying to stop you from taking that path, Beth. Don't you understand?"

Her breath came out in small pants, head up flung.

"All right, all right, I'll admit that I have never been certain of the permanency of Kim's love for me." The words were driven out reluctantly and she wondered wildly why she was voicing the fears that had so long been buried deep in her heart, but there was no getting away from this man. "But where does that get me? As you well know, love is no respecter of persons and I loved Kim, faults and all. I hate you, Ruan Trevelgen for making me say all this," her grey eyes darkening with anger.

"A much more healthy emotion, if I may say so, than the one you felt for Crudden."

Beth struggled against the strength of that hard tanned body as he held her firmly.

"Oh, let me go!" she said furiously.

"I wondered when you would really blow that copper topknot of yours," the dark pools rippling mockingly. "I expected some sort of explosion on that first day after my very rude remarks about you expecting to be waited on hand and foot." The dark head was shaken. "I was disappointed. All I got was polite indifference from those cool eyes of yours."

His hands fell away from her arms.

Beth picked up her towel with an angry flick that sent the sand in all directions and fled from him across the beach and up the steps.

There was a curious sense of suffering about the man as he watched her go, the sun coming out from behind a cloud to dapple the cliffs to a million colours. He had taken on the suffering of another. Something that had not happened to him for many years.

* * *

Mrs. Trevelgen made rapid progress and was so much better that she and Beth were able to take drives. Aunt May was as pleased as a child to be able to show Beth a little more of her beloved Cornwall, but when Beth suggested that it was time she looked for another post, Mrs. Trevelgen showed alarming signs of becoming really upset and Beth had to shelve her plans yet again.

The matter, however, was taken out of her hands in an unexpected way, by Dr. Jenkins. He rang her up one morning.

"Miss Dexter?"

"Yes."

"The hospital at St. Geraint is desperately short of a sister. I was wondering if you could help out there for a week, especially in view of the fact that your godmother is so much better. Of course, I would not have suggested this if it had been otherwise." His voice was crisp and Beth could picture the little doctor sitting at his desk, brown eyes, under fly-away brows, alert. She had a great deal of respect for him.

"I'd love to help out," she said quickly and made arrangements to see the Matron that afternoon. She replaced the receiver and went out to her godmother who was seated in her favourite place on the terrace.

Strangely enough, Mrs. Trevelgen made no objection when she heard Dr. Jenkins' request.

"That's different, dear child. I don't know why I didn't think of it myself and you'll be able to come to Truran House whenever you wish," and beamed happily up at Beth.

"Aunt May, I do believe you just kept me here so I wouldn't go off to London," Beth accused her.

"Well, dear child, you would have been very lonely up there and, whether you like it or not, I do have a sense of responsibility towards you. I'm sure if you went into a flat you wouldn't eat properly, young girls never do, but this idea of Dr. Jenkins' is perfect."

Beth found herself unable to resent this kindly, though arbitrary arranging of her affairs. For one so diminutive, her godmother had a remarkable knack of getting her own way, but after all, London wasn't the only place in which to find a job. One hospital was every bit as good as another and there was this lovely coast and countryside to explore in her free time.

* * *

Beth started work in the hospital at St. Geraint the following day, glad to be back in the strict routine where there was no time to brood and she felt happier than she had done for weeks.

The days flew by and Beth, coming

off duty one evening at the end of the week, found Ruan in the sitting room of the Nurses' Home.

"It's you," he said unnecessary, his eyes holding hers in a new awareness as they rested on her face and wings of copper hair beneath the prim white cap.

"Are you ready to come home."

"Yes, but just for a couple of days. I've been asked to stay on indefinitely."

Ten minutes later they were speeding along the road that led to the coast. The clouds that had dulled the day had rolled away, the sun turning the meadows and headland to a sheen of brilliant emerald.

"You are looking heaps better," said Ruan with a quick glance at the girl beside him, noting the serene grey eyes.

"I feel better, thank you." She smiled a little ruefully. "One realizes in a hospital, that there are people far worse off than you are and it has had a salutary effect on me. My troubles this week are trivial in comparison."

The sun dipped down over the horizon as they drove up the avenue, scattering its last moulten drops upon the cliff tops.

Ruan stopped the car in front of the house, but made no effort to get out.

"It's good to have you home again, Beth. We've missed you."

For a shattering moment, Beth knew that for the first time since she had arrived at Truran House, friendliness lay between this man and her, warm, comforting.

One by one the lights had gone on in the house facing the terrace and as Beth looked towards the house saw for a moment a silhoutted figure, dark against the lighted window of the diningroom and then it disappeared.

Sophia was not going to be pleased to see her back, even though it was only for a few days, thought Beth with a shiver.

★ ★ ★

Beth spent a happy day. Her godmother had brought up her breakfast at some ridiculously late hour and had stayed talking and when Beth had finally got up, they had driven into Penzance.

Just before tea, Beth came downstairs to find Sophia in the hall, the dark eyes fixed on her.

"So I see you've managed to prize the Trevelgen pearls from *Maman*," were her first words, her lips a thin disapproving line. "For services rendered, I presume. A handsome payment."

Beth's hands went to her throat coming to an abrupt halt in sheer astonishment.

Sophia came a step nearer, her fingers working spasmodically.

"Why should you have them? They belong to the family." Her voice was shrill.

"But — " Beth began, then gave a cry of distress. "Oh, they're broken." Her fingers had gone to the necklace in a protective movement and now the pearls lay scattered on the carpet and dark oak surrounds of the hall.

"That means tears," the elder woman said with vicious satisfaction, making no effort to help Beth, who had gone on her knees to pick them up.

Yes, thought Beth disconsolately. They did mean tears, for the pearls had been given to her by her parents, for her birthday, the day before they had met their tragic death.

Neither of them heard Ruan come in.

"What means tears," wondering what had caused the tenseness between the two women.

"Beth's just broken the Trevelgen pearls and what I want to know is, why *Maman* should give them to someone outside the family? Did you know about this, Ruan?" Sophia demanded.

"No, but if *Maman* wishes to do so, I've no objection, for she is still Mistress of Truran," he reminded her, "and Beth already has had her tears."

Sophia stared at Ruan, hating his

quiet reprimand, watching that head with its black hair so close to the copper one as he helped Beth pick up the pearls. With an angry exclamation she left them.

Beth laid the string on the small rosewood table, grading the beads carefully.

"I think they're all here," she said thankfully.

"But these aren't the Trevelgen pearls," said Ruan sharply. "That clasp is quite different. What on earth was Sophia making all the fuss about?"

"I tried to tell her, but she wouldn't listen," Beth said, upset by the incident.

Ruan was tying the pearls in his handkerchief.

"I'll see they are restrung for you," he said quietly, "and I'll go and tell Sophia she's made a mistake."

"Oh, how could she have thought I would accept a family heirloom," she said indignantly.

"Forget it! Sophia can get some strange ideas into her head on occasions."

After tea Ruan suggested a walk.

"And very nice too," beamed his mother, with an approving nod of her white head at Beth and watched them disappear through the door with tender eyes. "That child is not really beautiful," this to Sophia, "but she has something that lifts her out of the ordinary." Mrs. Trevelgen paused reflectively. "I can't quite place my finger on it. Good upbringing? Serenity?"

"I suppose you would like to see a match there?" said her daughter-in-law tartly.

Mrs. Trevelgen reached for her embroidery frame.

"I won't build up any hopes," then added slowly, "but for the first time in years, my son has become aware that women still exist and he is rather surprised, I think, at himself, to find the experience to his liking." The hazel eyes were amused.

With an expressive ejaculation Sophia

picked up a pile of plates and flounced from the room.

Mrs. Trevelgen smiled again, a small smile that just trembled her lips, the piece of tapestry falling to her lap. This house needed children — Ruan's children. Fancy him making Denzel his heir! Denzel was a dear little chap and she was very fond of her small grandson and wished that he had been sent to the local school, then there would have been child laughter here every day, but no, Sophia had insisted he be sent to that expensive school miles away. Her daughter-in-law could have waited until he was a little older, thought Mrs. Trevelgen wistfully.

★ ★ ★

Ruan and Beth walked along the headland until they reached the highest point overlooking Truran Village. From here they also had an excellent view of Truran House, standing four-square on its promontory, the sea battering the

214

cliff face below, gulls encircling Queen's Needle in courtship flight, the rock their mistress and Beth remembered how grim the huge stone house looked on that first morning as the mist wreathed its scarves of white and grey around its rough walls.

Ruan, in the main, was a silent companion, not given to small talk, but became quite eloquent when he got on to the subject of his birthplace, his deep blue eyes full of warmth and humour and Beth thought again he should smile more often, for in repose, his face suggested a stubborn, hard personality. She turned to see what had caught his attention. A man was coming along the cliff path.

"That's Inspector Tarica," he said. "I wonder if he's on duty, or enjoying the sunshine as we are," but there was an unease about him, quite out of keeping with the prosaic words.

The Inspector passed them with a wave of recognition and continued on his way to the village.

Beth enjoyed the walk up and over the headland, then half an hour later, they retraced their steps back to Truran House.

* * *

At dinner that evening, Ruan said:

"We saw Inspector Tarica on the cliff path this afternoon."

Sophia's reaction was that of a startled horse.

"Inspector Tarica?" her voice a little high as she demanded. "What's he snooping about for?" and Beth saw the sliver of fear in the dark eyes.

"Something to do with all these foreigners, I'll be bound," put in Maggie darkly, setting the big tureen of soup on the table.

Ruan picked up a spoon to serve it, unease a tangible sauce to the meal.

"Could be," he said noncommittally.

Sophia and that man on the cliff path. The memory shot into Beth's mind again, but she hurriedly steered

216

her thoughts in another direction. She was getting as bad as Maggie, but the next day something cropped up —

"Have you heard the story going around the village?" asked Maggie at lunch. Her look of enquiry turned to smug satisfaction when the family shook their heads. That she should be the bearer of a tit bit of news always pleased Maggie's gregarious soul.

"Well, it's a queer one, make no mistake. Old Jock is telling all and sundry that he's the Hound of Truran." Her bright eyes, under their sparse cover, watched for the family's reaction, defying them to say that it wasn't an interesting piece of gossip.

Sophia turned away impatiently, pulling off her jersey. "Oh, you know what Jock is. Surely, you're not going to believe what he says, are you?"

"But, Mistress Sophia," every line in that sagging body triumphant, "he says he was paid to do the job."

Now she had everyone's attention.

"Paid to do the job?" Ruan asked

sharply. "Are you sure he said that, Maggie? Paid to pretend to be the Hound?"

"Aye, and what's more it was with mine own ears, I heard it," she said with intense relish, hands on bulging hips.

"How could he possibly be the Hound. Nobody would believe that! He's just a simpleton," Sophia said, but her eyes were wary.

"There's more to it than that," Maggie went on, still big with news. "He says he was dared to climb Queen's Needle on the evening the Hound was seen."

"Using the Hound as a cover up! It's a well known fact that the fishing fleet won't go out if the Hound has been seen. Perfect for anyone wanting to run a cargo in at low tide," said Gawen, blue eyes darting from one startled face to another.

"Trust you to think up something like that," said Sophia. "Smuggling isn't carried out any longer."

"Do you think this is true, Maggie?" asked Ruan, with a keen glance at the old woman.

"Master Ruan, he has a new coat to show for it. One of those new fangled ones, long and shaggy."

"You mean that if he did climb Queen's Needle, he could well have been mistaken for the Hound, with the setting sun throwing him into relief?" said Ruan.

Maggie snorted.

"It only needs one person to think he's seen anything out of the ordinary and the whole village will swear that they have seen it too. Nobody likes to feel left out, like." The rich Cornish accent rolled out sagely, "but, aye, I think Jock, with that silly new coat of his, could have been mistaken for the Hound."

Ruan said no more, but a startled stare passed between the two brothers.

"But what for?" murmured Gawen. "Merely a dare?"

"We are always indebted to Maggie

for all our news," said Mrs. Trevelgen happily, her whole being radiating as intense an interest as Maggie's. Anything to do with the village was very close to her heart, but not for one moment did she believe a word of this farrago of nonsense. As Sophia had said, Jock was one of the simple ones and Mrs. Trevelgen knew what the villagers were like.

* * *

The next day, Ruan was able to add more to the story which he had found to be true. Old Jock Findley had climbed Queen's Needle the night the Hound had been seen.

"Yes," he said in answer to his mother's incredulity, "he really did climb the rock. Crouched there he would have certainly looked like the Hound. I also had a chat with Inspector Tarica and he said they had pulled in a foreigner the other evening for drunk and disorderly behaviour. It transpires he came over here illegally; was landed along the coast on that same night. The Inspector said the man appeared belligerent and bitter and wanted to be sent back."

Gawen's inquisitive blue eyes were suddenly shrewd.

"And poor simple Jock was the decoy. What a lucrative trade for someone," he said enviously. "Why didn't I think of it long ago?"

"You!" Scorn broke from Sophia like a breached dam, brown eyes hot, her thin mouth working. "You haven't an ounce of initiative in any part of you and as for exerting yourself — "

"Don't get so worked up, my dear," said Mrs. Trevelgen. "There's absolutely no need for it. I always say, getting worked up is not worth it. It churns up the stomach so," she added with a knowing nod at her daughter-in-law's averted head.

"What else did you hear?" asked Gawen keenly.

"They haven't caught the ring-leader

yet. Nobody is prepared to talk and you know how clannish people can get, especially as these foreigners are such good workers."

"So smuggling hasn't been wiped out," said Mrs. Trevelgen distastefully, "and this time it is human cargo."

It had been the morning following the appearance of the Hound that Gawen had been so off colour. Beth remembered with startling clarity, as she stood in front of her window, gazing out at Queen's Needle rearing out of the sea, a truly magnificent sentinel and focus point to Truran House. Had Sophia drugged her husband that night? Beth shied away from that unpleasant thought. No, Sophia would never do a thing like that, she tried to convince herself, but bringing in immigrants like that would mean a great deal of money, said a small inner voice and that was what Sophia badly needed, to make this estate a fitting inheritance for her son.

★ ★ ★

The weeks went by and Beth was still at the hospital at St. Geraint and it looked like becoming a permanent post. She spent most of her off duty at Truran House and had learnt to ignore Sophia's glowering dislike of her. One evening Gawen came in with a roll of paper under his arm, undid it then spread the sheet in front of his mother.

"How do you like the new designs, *Maman*?"

Beth leant over, surprise and pleasure filling her at the beautiful drawings displayed there.

"Wild flowers of Cornwall, I've called this series," said Gawen, not without pride.

"They're lovely, Gawen," said his mother and Beth agreed, studying the dainty tracery and delicate colours of the drawings.

"They should sell well," put in Sophia, the inevitable grey sock growing under her nimble fingers.

"I'd like to see the factory," Beth

said, but was caught up angrily by Sophia.

"It's not a factory. Each piece we turn out is hand made and painted."

"Like to go and see the pottery now?" asked Gawen. "I'd like Faulkner to see these drawings and we can call in there on our way back. By the way, he's one of our painters."

Beth and Gawen walked along a well worn, beech lined path, a squirrel or two peeping shyly from behind a barricade of spring foliage. The evenings had lengthened and it was very pleasant walking. A cluster of buildings came into view as the path took a turn.

"Here is the storeroom," said Gawen, unlocking the door and closing it behind him, switching on the light.

A musty smell hit them, but Beth went forward eagerly to look more closely at the beautiful china stored on rows and rows of wooden shelves.

"All the designs and shapes are excellent and such a high quality too." Beth was so used to the cheap china and ornaments that were turned out in ever increasing quantities in the Far East, that these articles in front of her gave her real pleasure.

"Did you think all this would be mass produced?" scoffed Gawen.

Beth nodded. "Something like that, until Sophia put me right." She picked up a figurine of a small boy on bended knee, looking up at — what? It was wholly charming, exquisite in line and colour.

Beth went from jugs to plates, from plaques to other novelties. Most of the items were painted, but one shelf was left for ornaments in terra cotta, the natural colour of the clay sufficient to give them an appeal of their own.

Beth was not conscious of the passing of time and was startled when Gawen said it was ten o'clock.

"We won't be able to go and see Faulkner."

"It's not as late as all that?" Beth gasped with a hurried glance at her watch.

225

"You shouldn't have been so interested, Beth," as they made their way between the shelves. He turned the handle of the door. He turned it again, but it resisted all his efforts to open it.

"Funny," he muttered, trying again, adding his weight to it. "I do believe we've been locked in," his mobile brows rising practically to his hairline, mouth drooping comically. "Now I wonder who can have done this and why?"

10

GAWEN tried again to open the door of the pottery storeroom, but was as unsuccessful as before, the pool of light thrown from the shaded bulb not quite reaching to where they stood.

"Didn't you bring in the key?" asked Beth with a frown.

"No, I'm sure I left it on the other side of the door," but he went through his pockets. "No, I haven't got it."

"Here, let me try," she said, but her efforts were no more successful than Gawen's had been. There was no mistake. It wasn't some prank being played by Gawen. They were well and truly locked in. "But this is silly," her laugh a little uneasy. "Gawen, you aren't playing tricks are you? You haven't got the key in your pocket?" she asked suspiciously.

"What me?" a little affronted.

"Yes, you," she said severely. "I wouldn't put it past you — not with that weird sense of humour of yours."

Gawen had hunched himself into a chair, his long, sensitive hands hanging between his knees, a frown on his usually cheerful face. He was still for a long time, then said slowly:

"I think Sophia is to blame for this little lark." He looked up at Beth, his eyes steady for once, no mischief lurking in those pale blue depths, the light picking out a stray white hair amongst the blackness. "She wants to get rid of you. Ruan has been too attentive of late. Oh yes, he has," seeing her swift movement of denial, "and Sophia is becoming scared." His lips had narrowed and a small pulse beat a tattoo at the angle of his jaw. "You'll have to make the best of it, Beth. We're locked in here for the night, if I'm not mistaken."

Beth could only stand and stare down at him. The situation, if what he said was true, was too ludicrous for words!

"If you had been some other man — "

"But there is no-one else to play off against Ruan," he took up swiftly.

Beth was suddenly angry.

"Don't you think Sophia will blame you?" she snapped.

"No, for I know how her mind works. She's trying to blacken your name, Beth, and make no mistake about it, every villager will hear about this."

Shocked disbelief darkened Beth's grey eyes.

"Using her own husband? Gawen, I don't believe you. Sophia would never sink to that level."

"You don't know my wife." His face was bleak. "She's not going to let anyone interfere with her plans for Denzel."

"But surely, if people knew we'd been locked in — "

"A likely story," he scoffed, "and as for saying Sophia did it — Oh yes, my wife has been very clever indeed." Something like a sneer touched the words. "As you say, who would believe that anyone, in their right senses, would lock up her husband with another woman. Oh no! I won't be blamed by her, she'll leave that to outsiders. I'm merely a means to an end. I've always known that."

For the first time since Beth had met this man, there was real emotion in his voice. She could feel the deep, humiliating, bitter hurt within him. Was it this hurt that made him live so vicariously through others, afraid to face life for himself?

"Beth, please leave soon. I honestly don't know what she'll do next. Sophia has this overriding ambition to keep Truran House for Denzel. It's become an obsession with her."

"But she'll become Mistress of Truran when Aunt May dies?"

"What if Ruan marries? This is what Sophia has been afraid of all these years, ever since Denzel was born. Ruan's a different person since you arrived, Beth." He paused and lit a cigarette, enhaling deeply, then letting the smoke trickle through his nostrils. "Sophia really wanted Ruan when we were young, but he was never interested. I was the besotted one."

What had drawn Gawen to Sophia? Beth had often wondered about this. Had he been conscious of the fact that the lack of drive in his own personality would be complemented by this woman's dominance and burning ambition?

Fear was a sudden taste far back in Beth's throat.

"I think Sophia's mad!" the words coming out with a shiver.

"No, but she will stop at nothing to get her own way. Watch her, Beth," gripping her arm. "She was absolutely furious when *Maman* told us you were coming here for a holiday."

Gawen looked a little old and very tired as he sat on the straight-back office chair.

"I mean it, Beth. I'm not fooling this time. You're too beautiful for Sophia's comfort," taking in the lovely line of cheek and jaw, the thickly lashed grey eyes and tawny head of hair.

"Well, the first thing is to get out of here," she said, going over to the small, frosted window.

"None of them open." Gawen hadn't even lifted his head.

Beth turned in surprise.

"Not any of them?"

He shook his head.

"This is a storeroom and when we built it, decided windows that didn't open would be a good burglar deterrent, hence also the small panes. Nobody can break one of those and get in."

" — and nobody can get out. Think of something, Gawen," she said urgently, coming back to shake him by the shoulders.

"My dear, there is no way out."

"Do you think someone will come and look for us?" she asked hopefully, after a leaden silence of minutes.

232

Gawen shrugged again.

"*Maman* will have gone to bed and Ruan doesn't know we came over here. That leaves my wife." The sneer was back again.

Beth glared at him.

"That's your trouble. You sit there instead of doing something. Another man would be prowling around, seeing if he could bash a hole in the ceiling and get out that way."

Beth's eyes suddenly glinted. "That gives me an idea. I'm not prepared to play your wife's silly games," and before he knew what she was about, Beth had picked up a chair and broken several panes of frosted glass. "Now turn that light switch off and on, Gawen," authoritatively. "Someone is bound to see it and come and investigate. If Sophia, or anyone else, thinks they can do this to me, they're mistaken."

A gleam of amusement, not unmixed with admiration lit Gawen's pale blue eyes as he made his way to the door. What a girl, he thought with wry humour. He wouldn't have thought to break a window. Good luck to Ruan and, for the first time in his life, envied his brother.

It was at least an hour before a shaggy head, with a startled face, peered in at the jagged window of the storeroom.

"Wot's going on in 'ere? Why, Master Gawen!" mouth agape.

"Jock," Gawen cried. "Man, am I glad to see you! Beth, this is the fellow who thought he was the Hound." He gave a chuckle.

"I am the Hound of Truran," the old man corrected him proudly, his eyes glinting weirdly in that wrinkled face. He gathered his tattered garments around him as if they were the royal robes themselves.

"And what happened to your new coat?" asked Gawen.

Jock leaned a little closer to the window, grubby fingers taking hold of the bars. One eye closed slowly.

"Sold it," he whispered succinctly.

"Got a lot of money for it, I did."

"You'll get some more, you old rascal, if you do as I say."

The old head was cocked eagerly.

"All I want you to do is go around to the door and see if the key is in the lock. Do you understand?"

"Aye, Master Gawen. I'll do that for a couple of bob. Nice and easy it'll be too."

They could hear his shuffling gait, scuffing the loose stones as he walked around to the front of the building, muttering to himself. He was soon back, his face once more peering in at the smashed window.

"Well, did you get the key?" asked Gawen quickly.

Old Jock's stare was half vacant, half crafty.

"Do I get another coat?"

"The key, man! The key!"

"What key, Master Gawen?"

Gawen turned away with an impatient exclamation.

"Please, Jock," Beth said quietly.

"See if the key is still in the door. If it's there, bring it to me. I don't want to stay here all night. It's cold."

"Aye, I'll go and see for you, Mistress." The old eyes were now docile.

He reappeared after what seemed an age, shaking his unkempt head of black and silver hair.

"It's not there. Old Jock had a good look."

"I thought it wouldn't be," Gawen said coming back to the window. "Jock, go and fetch Ruan."

"Where's my money?" the old one muttered.

"You'll get it as soon as you have fetched Master Ruan and Jock, I don't want Mistress Sophia, or the Mistress Trevelgen or Maggie, but Master Ruan. Do you understand?"

"Aye!" The one word held a wealth of meaning. "Master Ruan would want to rescue the Mistress of Truran himself," a strange light in the sunken eyes as they rested on Beth. "But she'll be all right with you, Master Gawen. You've never hurt a thing in your life, not even a rabbit in the field, or a fish from the stream."

"But I'm not — " Beth began.

"Oh leave it," said Gawen impatiently again. "Jock, we are locked in and don't want to spend the night here. Go, you fool and hurry. Bring Ruan. Bring him here and tell him to bring a key," he added.

The bent figure disappeared from the pool of light.

"Do you really think he understands?" asked Beth, sitting down.

"Heaven alone knows!"

When Ruan arrived, Beth had never seen anyone so coldly angry.

"Sophia, I suppose?" were his first words as he opened the door.

"How did you know?" his brother asked.

Ruan stood there, an old-fashioned lantern in his hand, its wick burning amber red, its rays casting shadows under the high cheek bones and well

237

shaped nose, his eyes reflecting their dark anger.

"She was in the hall when I came in and seemed ill at ease. I didn't take much notice at the time, but when Jock arrived and told me you were both locked in the pottery storeroom, I knew."

The short walk back was covered in silence, the lantern throwing a jerky spread of light at each step Ruan took, the trees on either side of the path close and tall. Beth shivered, glad not to be walking this road alone. Sophia was in the hall as they came in.

"You must have found the pottery extremely interesting for you to have stayed out so late," with a suggestive glance at her watch, then at Beth.

"Enough!" said Ruan. His voice matched the cold, hard lines of his jaw. "There will be no place for you under my roof, Sophia, if you ever do such a thing again."

"What am I supposed to have done?" she demanded, but as Ruan strode into the study without replying, fear filled the dark eyes and the shoulders under the brown silk blouse slumped suddenly.

"If you hadn't come here, Beth Dexter, this wouldn't have happened."

The following week, Beth was again at Truran House. Ruan, as usual, had brought her across from St. Geraint. She looked around her room with pleasure, then changed quickly out of her uniform into a frock of wild silk that had been made for her by one of Ah Wing's numerous relations. The shot pattern of blues, mauves and pinks suited her grey eyes and brought out the tawny lights of her hair.

Beth hurried downstairs. Dinner had been brought forward as Ruan was taking the night train to London.

"I've put the coffee in the lounge, Ma'am," said Maggie, when the meal had ended.

"Thank you," said Mrs. Trevelgen. "We'll go through now."

Beth stopped, poised in the act of

entering the room. Gawen had turned on the radio and the haunting strains of the tune made her stiffen. She turned blindly and went out on to the terrace, leaning against the sunwarmed stone parapet, needing its support for her suddenly weak legs.

The song went on, Beth did not even know its name, but she was back in Singapore, the events of the last six months crowding in on her. Dancing in Kim's arms, her parents' tragedy and the awful weeks that followed it, when hope had died, a slow torturous death; saying goodbye to Ah Wing, with the sure knowledge she would never see her old *amah* again. Kim and Fen —

All this swept through her with a nostalgia so great that it nearly overwhelmed her, highlighting a loneliness of the soul that now had her in its grip and with aching poignancy that loneliness could be a bitter sauce to memory.

Her hands gripped the grey stone until her knuckles stood out white, unaware that Ruan had come up behind her and only when he gently took her by the arms and pulled her against him, did she start a little.

Beth leaned against the broad wall of his chest for the space of a heartbeat, closing her eyes, her senses excruciatingly alive to his nearness, the hard feel of his hands on her arms through the soft silk of her frock, his warm breath on the nape of her neck. She was conscious of his more rapid breathing and never in her life had she felt such a furious pang of longing and uncontrolled need to be loved and to love somebody. A faint betraying shiver went through her.

Somebody? Anybody? That was not love and drew away sharply.

"There's no going back, Beth — ever — in time or reason," Ruan said quietly. Those memory-haunted eyes had hurt him, grey eyes that had met his only fleetingly.

"No," she conceded ruefully, "but there are moments, a tune, a perfume, the shape of a head, when memory plays impish tricks."

Ruan was standing beside her now, comfortingly close, the evening breeze lifting her hair and blowing it across his face. He put up a hand to imprison its silky strands and knew this girl had woven herself into the very fabric of his being, quietly, unobstrusively and his senses soared. He was alive again and found it an exhilarating experience. The years the locusts had eaten had fallen away as if they had never been.

Sophia stood in the doorway, naked venom on her face, watching those two close figures and then Beth became aware of her and the spell was broken.

"Gawen is waiting to take you to the station," Sophia said sourly.

Beth helped with the washing up. Sophia had muttered that she had a headache and had disappeared upstairs. The woman looked ill and the nervous twitch at the side of her mouth had worsened of late. She should see a doctor, thought Beth, hanging up the tea towel and then went back into the lounge where a small fire was burning, for the evening was chilly.

"Ruan will find it cold on the train," she said, seating herself beside her godmother. "Train!" The word came out jerkily. "What date is it?" her breath rasping through her lips as if she had run a great distance.

Mrs. Trevelgen looked at her with surprise, startled at the urgency of the girl beside her.

"Either the 29th or 30th. I'm not sure myself. Does it matter all that much, dear child?"

"Where is a calendar?" Beth's mind had gone a blank.

"There's one in the office."

Beth rushed out of the room and across the hall, throwing open the door of the small room. There on the desk stood a calendar, its black numbers screaming at her. It was the 30th of June.

A nightmare quality invaded Beth,

buckling her knees and making her feel sick.

Her dream that she had had on the plane whilst on her way to this country, had taken her forward in time, for in that dream, the hurrying figure she had been trying to stop from boarding a train, was someone she dearly loved. Tonight Beth knew, beyond a shadow of doubt, that it was Ruan. She had wondered, that day of her arrival, why the back of his head had looked so familiar, with the black hair growing deep into his neck.

The love she had had for Kim paled into insignificancy beside this deep, overwhelming emotion that now shook her to the very depths of her being and it caught her off guard. Was she so fickle minded that she could love two men in so short a time? But this was different. The torment of insecurity had stalked side by side with her love for Kim.

"Ruan!" His name burst from her. He would be on that train.

Her cry of horror brought Mrs. Trevelgen hurrying to the door.

"What on earth's the matter, Beth? You tore out of the lounge as if a devil were at your heels." She caught Beth's arm. "Why, child, you're as white as a sheet."

"It's the 30th of June," gasped Beth, pointing to the calendar. "Ruan must not go by that train tonight."

Mrs. Trevelgen glanced across the hall to where the grandfather clock stood.

"It's too late anyway. He's on already. The train, as you know, leaves at 7.30 and it is that now. What is this all about?" The sharp note of authority sat strangely on this small woman.

Beth, sinking limply into a chair, told her of her dream, grey eyes wide with recaptured memory. Her terrifying inability to reach the man, the train leaving the station and then the jumble of coaches along a high embankment, the date — 30th June.

"Get him off, Aunt May," she pleaded, catching her godmother by the arm, her face bleak and drawn. "He'll be killed."

Mrs. Trevelgen drew Beth to her, holding the copper head close in her shoulder, trying to blot out the terror in that voice, feeling the tenseness of the young shoulders under the silk frock.

"Darling, it was only a dream," she said soothingly, "and how do you know it was Ruan? You had never met him until you came here."

Beth drew away in a fever of exasperation.

"Of course I did not know at the time," she said. "I only saw the back of his head, but it was Ruan, Aunt May, I know it was. Oh, please do something," beating a clenched fist into the palm of her hand.

"You really believe this dream will come true, don't you?" Mrs. Trevelgen was regarding her goddaughter with a tolerant air, not unmixed with kindness.

"It was so vivid. Please do something."

"But what, dear child?" her godmother asked with a dawning anxiety as Beth's fear began to transmit itself to her. "One can't just stop a train."

"Ring up the next station and say you're ill. Ruan must come home."

"But I'm not ill and I shudder to think what Ruan would say if he were hauled off the train, merely for the whims of two women."

There was a silence in the cabinet-lined room, the tick of the grandfather clock in the hall slow and loud, each metronomic measure beating mercilessly on Beth's brain, taking Ruan further away from her.

'Oh, please don't let him be on that train. Please,' she silently prayed. 'How could I live without you. Ruan! Ruan!'

"I suppose you're right, Aunt May," Beth said at last. "I can well imagine Ruan's comments if he were asked to leave the train because of a silly dream." A small chuckle escaped her uneasily. "He really would go mad."

Words, words! She was merely trying to mask her inner perturbation as she remembered the rest of her horrifying dream. The scatter of derailed carriages along a high embankment as if thrown there by some careless hand.

★ ★ ★

Gawen arrived back a little later.

"You're back early," said his mother with surprise, her white head coming around as he entered the room.

"I didn't wait to see Ruan off. Dropped him this side of St. Geraint. Said he'd walk the rest of the way seeing it was early. Any coffee going?"

"I'll get some," said Beth hurriedly, glad of the opportunity to make her escape.

"You're a little pale," said Gawen, with one of his keen stares, when she brought the coffee through into the lounge.

Beth was grateful to her godmother

for not having said anything about her dream.

"I must be losing some of my Singapore tan," she was able to retort lightly. "Now you're seeing what's underneath."

Gawen grinned.

"You still look all right to me."

Sophia had joined them and Beth poured her out a cup of coffee. She still looked wretched, but said her headache was better.

"Hello," said Gawen, his cup half way to his mouth, his pale blue eyes filled with curiosity. "I hear a car coming up the drive. Are we expecting visitors?"

"Probably someone who has lost his way," said Sophia. "You really should replace that 'No through road' sign, Gawen. The amount of motorists who have to turn back!"

They all were startled when the front door was heard to open then close and before anyone could move to see who it was taking such liberties with their front door, Ruan entered the room.

Beth had not been aware of holding her breath until his voice broke the tension, but there was a curious lack of expression about him as he said:

"Missed that darned train!"

"Ruan?" Beth said tentatively, as if she did not believe he really stood there, unable to take her eyes from his face. Her prayer had been answered, or was this yet another dream?

"You were going to say?" For once there was no mockery about him, only a half angry, half rueful expression in those dark blue eyes.

"No — nothing." Beth turned hurriedly away from that glance, colour rushing to her pale cheeks. He was safe, relief a spice far back on her tongue.

Gawen's eyebrows had skyed.

For once, the meaning of the under-currents which he could feel surging around, were eluding him and, in some vague way, it annoyed him.

"You'll have to ring Maxwell and go up on tomorrow's train," said Sophia prosaically, "but how you came to miss that train — "

"You had plenty of time," cut in Gawen.

"My watch must have been slow." Ruan's whole manner was evasive. "Anyway, I missed it." He appeared abstracted and disinclined to talk.

Beth could stand no more.

"I must get to bed," she said hurriedly.

"Just wait until the news, dear child," said her godmother, "and I'll come up with you. Gawen please switch on the radio, dear."

They sat around in silence, Sophia knitting, Gawen sketching on the back of his cigarette box, while Ruan read the paper he had bought at the station kiosk, but Beth saw he had been staring at the same page for a considerable time.

The news came over and then the announcer said:

"Here's a special news item just to hand. The connection from St. Geraint was derailed six miles from Povey. It is thought that casualties are heavy."

But it couldn't have happened, thought Beth wildly. Dreams don't come true.

Sophia's knitting was stilled, her eyes darkened with shock.

"I won't have a moment's peace now. Gawen, you'll have to fetch Denzel from school and take him back. I can't have him travelling any more by that train. Gawen!" she said sharply. "Did you hear me?" Forgotten was the fact that her brother-in-law was to have been on that train; her only thought was for her son.

Gawen, for once shocked into silence, said resignedly:

"Yes, my dear. I heard you."

Mrs. Trevelgen had crumpled, her face, fragile as old china, working pitiably. Was it love that had cheated death, she wondered, with a feeling of deep indebtedness to her godchild. Had her love kept Ruan from catching that train? She pulled herself together and saw that Beth was staring wildly at Ruan.

"What a lucky escape you had," said Gawen, words Mrs. Trevelgen had been about to utter, but Ruan had not heard for he was holding Beth's eyes with his own.

Gawen was again conscious of an indefinable something between these two that he could not understand.

Abruptly Ruan stood up.

"I think we should go. I know Beth will be invaluable and Povey is not so far away."

* * *

Ruan, Gawen and Beth were soon speeding along the country lanes, Beth wedged close to Ruan's shoulder as all three sat in front of the car. They turned a corner, then stared.

"Good Lord!" muttered Gawen.

Coaches were scattered along the railway line like toys a child had emptied out of a box, but Beth had a fleeting sense of relief. The accident in her dream had been ten times worse than this one, but it was bad enough.

The next hours were confusion. Beth attached herself to a knot of medical staff working over the injured and dying, while Ruan and Gawen helped release the trapped. There seemed to be no end to the night.

It was near dawn when the last casualty was taken away to hospital. Beth was exhausted and slipped thankfully on to the seat of the car, Ruan following soon after, coat torn, face blackened and a scratch of congealed blood along the cheek nearest to her.

They sat in silence for a long time.

"I could have been in all that," he said grimly. "Beth, I — ", turning abruptly to her, but broke off as Gawen appeared at the door.

"What I need is a stiff drink," he said, banging it behind him with a savage movement, running a hand tiredly over his face. "Let's go home."

When Ruan, Beth and Gawen arrived

back at Truran House, they found Mrs. Trevelgen and Sophia up, anxiously awaiting news of the disaster.

"Let me get a drink inside of me first," said Gawen, crossing to the cabinet.

"I'm sure you'd all like some coffee," said Mrs. Trevelgen, pouring out three cups from a big flask on the sideboard. "Was it very bad, Beth?"

"Yes," she said soberly, gratefully accepting the hot beverage. "The darkness didn't help either, although there were a few lights where we were working."

"Drink up quickly, dear, and go and have a hot bath. You all look fagged to death."

"Beth's used to this sort of thing, *Maman*," Sophia said evenly.

"One never gets used to this sort of thing, as you so callously put it," Beth said hotly, "and now, please excuse me," placing the cup on the tray as she passed. "Goodnight."

Ruan lifted his head and made a

movement as if to follow her, but changed his mind, sinking back into his chair. He was distrait and had not said a word since they had come in.

Beth crossing the hall heard Gawen say:

"Cheer up, old chap. You should be on top of the world. You could have been in that mess up." He had already recovered all his old buoyancy.

Beth had her bath and was going along the passage, tiredness in every limb, when Ruan crossed the gallery and saw her.

"Beth!"

She noticed he had washed and the cut on his cheek had been dressed.

"The bathroom's free," was all she could find to say. "I'm sorry I've taken such an age."

"Beth, I must talk to you," urgency roughing his voice. "Come into *Maman*'s sitting room." He took her towel and toilet bag from her unresisting hand and put them on the small, halfmoon table just inside the room.

"I'd better go and get dressed," she said a little self-consciously, but he waved aside her suggestion impatiently, going over to stand in front of the fire, now only grey ashes, after he had seen her seated in the comfortable chintz-covered chair.

"Do you know how I came to miss that train? Do you?" he demanded. "We used to burn witches in the old days for much less."

Beth looked up startled into the strong, tanned face, meeting eyes that held a curious tenderness, for it was mixed with accusation. Was he suggesting that she had been instrumental in him missing that connection for the London Express? It was impossible!

"It wasn't like you said — your watch was slow?" she asked tentatively, grey eyes wide and enquiringly.

Ruan shook his head, the light from the small chandelier, burnishing it to an ebony blackness.

"No, I was on the platform in good time and was just about to board the train. In fact, my foot was already on the step — " he paused. "Beth, you aren't going to believe this, that is why I said my watch was slow, but I've got to tell you. Suddenly, there you were."

Beth pressed her fingers to her lips to stop them trembling.

"Silly, isn't it? But it was you all right and Beth, you had such a look of horror and fear on your face as you turned to me that I — I started after you. Well, why don't you laugh? I told you it was silly, didn't I?"

It was very still in the room, dawn's light already creeping into the room.

"No, I'll not laugh," Beth said quietly. "There's just an immense thankfulness taking possession of me."

"It wasn't you there, was it, Beth? I mean you were here at Truran House all evening?"

Beth could only nod her head.

"I thought you must have been," he muttered and then went on hurriedly as if what he was about to say, still didn't make sense.

"The platform was crowded. I pushed past people, trying to reach you, but you were always just out of reach. You — oh, I know it's fantastic," half turning to stare down at the dead fire. "Can you wonder I could not tell my family the truth. It would give Gawen fuel for that weird sense of humour of his, that would last for months."

Ruan straightened up, his glance going to the girl curled up in the big chair, noticing the small bare feet peeping out from underneath her gown, the grey eyes huge as she waited for him to continue.

"I got to the end of the platform, but you had disappeared, and when I came to my senses the train was far down the line and I was left standing there like a gaupus, with old Mattick, the Station Master, grinning all over his scraggy face. It was as if, for once, he had got some of his own back, for the many times Gawen and I had played tricks on him as young lads. I was absolutely livid with myself, as you can well imagine and it was fortunate that I had time to cool down before reaching home. It didn't improve matters, though, seeing you sitting there, as if you'd seen a ghost. I've never seen such heartfelt relief on anyone's face before. Then came that news item — "

He grew silent, his hand going to his pocket for his cigarette case.

"What time did the train leave?" Beth asked in a small voice. She had to know.

"Seven thirty," he said, absurdly disappointed at the prosaic question, when there was a dozen other more important ones to be asked, "and on the dot for a change. Why?"

"But I didn't know before that time that it was the 30th," she said confusedly.

Ruan stared down at her.

"What on earth are you talking about?"

Beth shivered and pulled her warm gown more tightly around her slim body.

"What I'm about to tell you, Ruan, is as far-fetched as that which you have just told me."

He had seated himself next to her, throwing away his newly lit cigarette.

"On the plane coming over, I had a dream. I was also running along a platform, through a crowd of people, just as you did earlier on this evening, getting nowhere. I had to stop a man from getting on the train. Only the back of his head was visible, so I never knew who it was — until tonight." The last words were barely audible. "In my dream that man actually boarded the train and when it had pulled out of the station, I looked up at the clock. On it was written, in bold black letters, the 30th June and then I saw the derailment."

Beth felt, rather than saw, Ruan's start of surprise.

"It was much worse than the one tonight. Not one carriage had been spared." She shivered. "It was terrible!"

"So you willed me to stay off that train this evening," he said slowly.

"But, Ruan, it was 7.30 by the hall clock when I remembered my dream. The train must have been leaving."

"That clock always gains a bit. Strange! How is it possible for a person to get through to another, like you did tonight? The only answer is so improbable that it borders on the fantastic — to me, anyway." He turned around in his chair to face her.

Beth smiled, a wide friendly smile that started on her lips and crept to her eyes.

"And what is the answer?"

"That you love me, Beth," he said with a finality that left no denial. "A love so strong that it even protects at a distance."

Colour swept in her pale cheeks. His

reply had been wholly unexpected.

"Oh, Ruan, please," she pleaded, getting up hurriedly from her chair, her toes fumbling for her slippers. "Please don't let's go into that now. Too much has already happened today."

"Perhaps you're right," he conceded and leaning down, he lightly brushed her lips with his own. "Thank you, Beth."

A warm friendly act, but she found her heart was beating uncontrollably, her lips quivering.

Beth stood for a long time at her window and saw a tall figure walking the sands, the moon, in the pale sky, a silver horn still dispensing light for the goddess of the departed night. A tender smile touched her mouth and wondered if she was to find safe harbourage at last.

Beth slept late and when she did finally go downstairs, was almost relieved to find that Ruan would not be in for lunch. A shyness had made her somewhat loath to come face to face with him, with so much left unsaid between them.

That afternoon Beth slipped a coat over her cotton frock, tied a scarf over her head and went down the stairs. Her godmother had practically shooed her out of the house.

"Go, my dear. A walk will do you good after last night. I'm going to turn out the linen cupboard."

"Do you think you should?" Beth asked doubtfully.

"After I've had my rest, yes." Her hazel eyes twinkled. "Now off you go, dear child."

Beth walked along the headland, the wind cold on her cheeks, whipping her loose coat around her bare legs, but she found it exhilarating. She walked briskly for some time then decided it was time to turn back, but paused, gazing in delight at the sea, the sun shimmering silver on the outgoing tide, fussy little waves kneading the sands below.

As Beth turned to go back, she

noticed that someone else was sharing the headland with her this lovely afternoon and as the figure drew nearer, coming along the narrow path through gorse and stubbly grass, saw it was Sophia.

"Aren't the cliffs beautiful this afternoon," was Beth's greeting.

"Everything is lovely for you, isn't it?" The lack of emotion in the woman was uncanny, the sharp features devoid of expression, except for the eyes. A fanatical light lurked in their deep darkness. "Why didn't you go to London? Things would have been so different." It was as if she was talking to herself.

A chill feathered Beth's skin.

"It's too late now." The still face twisted suddenly. "It's too late," Sophia said again, on a rising note of hysteria.

Somehow, to the watching girl, the whole situation had changed dramatically. Something horrible and sinister was engulfing her as her eyes were drawn mesmerically to the elder woman.

"Even if you did leave the neighbourhood now, Ruan would follow you."

Sophia had scrambled over the loose boulders and was now standing on the edge of the cliff.

"Sophia," Beth said quietly, following her. "I'm going back. Coming?" A terrible panic was beginning to grip her, holding her by the throat, forcing her breath inwards.

Sophia turned, seemingly unaware of the fact that one false step would send her hurtling to the rocks below.

"You shall not have Ruan, do you hear?" Her voice cracked with jealous fury. "You'll not have Truran House."

"You're ill, Sophia. Let me take you home."

Sophia's laugh was ugly, a choking sound that bubbled in her throat and Beth's heart gave a terrified lurch.

"No, I'm not ill, or mad. I just know what I want. Truran House is for Denzil. Before you came here, Ruan never looked at another woman, but you, with your soft ways and lovely figure, have made him quite daft." She was panting now as she faced Beth, demented hatred in every line of her ravaged, jerking body.

"Sophia, don't tear yourself like this," pleaded Beth. "Ruan and I are only friends."

"Of course he loves you. Haven't I watched him look at you with his soul in his eyes. After all these years, he has fallen in love again. If he hasn't told you, it is because he thinks it is too soon after your break with Kim." She paused, then spat out with malicious satisfaction. "That young doctor jilted you properly, didn't he?" Her mouth trembled suddenly. "He shouldn't have done it, Beth. Why did he do it? He should have married you and taken you away from Truran House, away from Ruan. I should have stopped Fenella."

Beth could almost see her devious mind working out what she should have done, but it was too late.

"You cannot treat people like chess pieces," Beth said, a desperate fear pricking the back of her skull. "Come, Sophia, let's go home," holding out a pleading hand.

"Home? So that's how you regard Truran House? So Ruan has asked you to be his wife. I thought there was something between you last night."

"No, he hasn't, Sophia, if that will make you any happier."

Sophia stood there on the edge of the cliff, a tall, well-built figure that cast a long shadow on the turf.

"He will and do you think I'd let a chit like you stand in the way of all my plans? You have everything I have ever wanted. Beauty, Ruan's love, the chance of being Mistress of Truran House and your son — I hate you!" A high scream bubbled out, the wind carrying the words away, her face a twisted white mask, the skin taut over the cheek bones.

Sophia was trembling violently, her

hands working convulsively and then she made a lunge at Beth, catching her by the shoulders, her face thrust close.

"You shall not marry him, do you hear!"

Ice cold apprehension turned to frozen terror as she caught a glimpse of the ragged rocks below. The sight and the thought that her body would any moment land on those barbarous points like some ancient sacrifice, loosened her limbs and she began to struggle.

Sophia was surprisingly strong and Beth found herself slowly, but exorably inched towards the precipice. Just when she felt sure they would both go over the cliff face, Sophia loosened her hold and fell to the ground writhing on the coarse grass, holding her hands in front of her as if warding off some terrible danger that was threatening her throat.

It was some seconds before Beth, laying spent and breathless, became aware of what Sophia was screaming. All Beth knew was a great, overriding relief washing through her, the terror that had engulfed her receding, her breath still coming in great gulps.

"Shag!" Sophia screamed again. "Don't! Let go, Shag!" still making ineffectual movements with her hands, her screams mingling with the cry of the gulls.

Throwing off this new hypnotising horror, Beth quickly went over to where the elder woman lay.

"Sophia!" she called desperately, her hands trying to still the troubled body, but the writhings and twistings went on.

"Call off Shag," she gasped, her lips drawing back in a distorted grimace, her words coming out as if there was a great weight on her chest making speech difficult.

Beth's eyes widened incredulously.

"Shag?" her voice trembled over the name, but she was willing to try anything to stop this dreadful fit. "Shag!"

Sophia lay still, her head lolling

to one side, her breathing rapid and shallow and then she slowly rose to her feet, her clothes dishevelled, her face contorted beyond recognition.

"I'll go. I'll go," she muttered, her eyes still like that of a wild animal. "I know when I'm beaten," and stumbled along the cliff path.

Beth watched her run across the headland, a pathetic, unbalanced creature, whose high jangle of laughter floated to her.

★ ★ ★

Beth lay on the turf, her face buried in her arms, the menacing terrors of the past few minutes ebbing away, her whole body suspended in a void of relief so intense that for a moment she did not hear Ruan's shout.

He had watched the whole drama that had been enacted on the cliff top the two struggling figures locked in a deadly embrace, some inner sense telling him it could only be Beth

271

and Sophia, powerless to do anything, except run, run as he had never run before. He had shouted without any hope of being heard; saw both figures fall to the ground, horror and a terrible fear mounting within him.

"Beth, are you all right?"

She sat up, startled, but this wasn't the Ruan she knew, this white, haggard man who quickly knelt and passionately, desperately, pulled her into his arms, with a longing blended with a kind of sick horror. He pushed her head against him to smother the shock and distress he saw mirrored in the grey eyes. They hurt him unbearably.

Beth was still shivering violently, then the tension snapped and she began to weep, great gulping sobs that went on and on.

Ruan held her until the sobbing quietened down.

"Thank God you're all right," he muttered into the silky hair.

"At one stage I thought you both would go over."

"Shag saved me," but was it Shag, wondered Beth. She would never know. It could have been a fit, the heaviness in Sophia's chest and her disordered brain making her think a dog had tackled her.

Ruan put her gently away from him, the dark blue eyes worried.

"I think all this has been too much for you. Shag is our family ghost, remember?"

But Beth shook her head, safe and secure now in his arms.

"I'm all right, Ruan and it did look very much as if Sophia was fighting something. She kept trying to ward it off with her hands and calling his name." Beth shivered again. "She needs medical attention."

Ruan gathered her to him again as the sensitive face began to quiver.

"Beth, my darling, it's all over."

"But I can't forget. Oh, Ruan, I can't. She blamed me for everything; said I was a threat to Denzel's inheritance."

His mouth was grim.

"I think I should tell you that Inspector Tarica has been at the house. It seems that it was Sophia who organised this illegal entry of immigrants into the country. I was on my way to find her. That's why I saw you."

"Oh, Ruan, no!" whispered Beth, with deep distress, her arms tightening around him, her body acting bastion to what all this would mean to the Master of Truran and the whole family — her godmother, Gawen. "And Gawen?" The question came out hesitantly.

"No, he's not implicated. Gawen would never do a thing like that." Ruan paused. "Perhaps, in a way, I'm to blame for all this. Sophia began building impossible dreams when I made Denzel my heir."

He tilted her face to his.

"I hadn't met you then, Beth. I love you, darling. Could you take a man, who has wasted years living off husks and make him yours?"

Beth's grey eyes were tender.

"Yes, I could, because I love you too, Ruan. It is strange, that in my dream, I loved you and I hadn't even met you then. I only realized it that night of the train accident. Why, it was only last night," she said with startled amazement. "I feel as if I've lived a life time this afternoon."

"Oh no, you haven't," said Ruan, hauling her to her feet. "That life time belongs to me, my darling." His kiss was long and tender.

As Ruan and Beth walked home close together, Beth had a strange sensation that a third walked beside them and smiled a little at the fanciful thought that a cold nose had just been thrust against her bare leg.

THE END

WITH SOMEBODY ELSE
Theresa Charles

Rosamond sets off for Cornwall with Hugo to meet his family, blissfully unaware of the shocks in store for her.

A SUMMER FOR STRANGERS
Claire Hamilton

Because she had lost her job, her flat and she had no money, Tabitha agreed to pose as Adam's future wife although she believed the scheme to be deceitful and cruel.

VILLA OF SINGING WATER
Angela Petron

The disquieting incidents that occurred at the Vatican and the Colosseum did not trouble Jan at first, but then they became increasingly unpleasant and alarming.

DOCTOR NAPIER'S NURSE
Pauline Ash

When cousins Midge and Derry are entered as probationer nurses on the same day but at different hospitals they agree to exchange identities.

A GIRL LIKE JULIE
Louise Ellis

Caroline absolutely adored Hugh Barrington, but then Julie Crane came into their lives. Julie was the kind of girl who attracts men without even trying.

COUNTRY DOCTOR
Paula Lindsay

When Evan Richmond bought a practice in a remote country village he did not realise that a casual encounter would lead to the loss of his heart.

ENCORE
Helga Moray

Craig and Janet realise that their true happiness lies with each other, but it is only under traumatic circumstances that they can be reunited.

NICOLETTE
Ivy Preston

When Grant Alston came back into her life, Nicolette was faced with a dilemma. Should she follow the path of duty or the path of love?

THE GOLDEN PUMA
Margaret Way

Catherine's time was spent looking after her father's Queensland farm. But what life was there without David, who wasn't interested in her?

HOSPITAL BY THE LAKE
Anne Durham

Nurse Marguerite Ingleby was always ready to become personally involved with her patients, to the despair of Brian Field, the Senior Surgical Registrar, who loved her.

VALLEY OF CONFLICT
David Farrell

Isolated in a hostel in the French Alps, Ann Russell sees her fiancé being seduced by a young girl. Then comes the avalanche that imperils their lives.

NURSE'S CHOICE
Peggy Gaddis

A proposal of marriage from the incredibly handsome and wealthy Reagan was enough to upset any girl — and Brooke Martin was no exception.

A DANGEROUS MAN
Anne Goring

Photographer Polly Burton was on safari in Mombasa when she met enigmatic Leon Hammond. But unpredictability was the name of the game where Leon was concerned.

PRECIOUS INHERITANCE
Joan Moules

Karen's new life working for an authoress took her from Sussex to a foreign airstrip and a kidnapping; to a real life adventure as gripping as any in the books she typed.

VISION OF LOVE
Grace Richmond

When Kathy takes over the rundown country kennels she finds Alec Stinton, a local vet, very helpful. But their friendship arouses bitter jealousy and a tragedy seems inevitable.

CRUSADING NURSE
Jane Converse

It was handsome Dr. Corbett who opened Nurse Susan Leighton's eyes and who set her off on a lonely crusade against some powerful enemies and a shattering struggle against the man she loved.

WILD ENCHANTMENT
Christina Green

Rowan's agreeable new boss had a dream of creating a famous perfume using her precious Silverstar, but Rowan's plans were very different.

DESERT ROMANCE
Irene Ord

Sally agrees to take her sister Pam's place as La Chartreuse the dancer, but she finds out there is more to it than dyeing her hair red and looking like her sister.